By Stephen Mitchell

POETRY

Parables and Portraits

FICTION

The Frog Prince

Meetings with the Archangel

NONFICTION

The Gospel According to Jesus

TRANSLATIONS AND ADAPTATIONS

Real Power: Business Lessons from the Tao Te Ching
(with James A. Autry)

Full Woman, Fleshly Apple, Hot Moon:
Selected Poems of Pablo Neruda

Genesis

Ahead of All Parting:
The Selected Poetry and Prose of Rainer Maria Rilke

A Book of Psalms

The Selected Poetry of Dan Pagis

Tao Te Ching

The Book of Job

The Selected Poetry of Yehuda Amichai *(with Chana Bloch)*

The Sonnets to Orpheus

The Lay of the Love and Death of Cornet Christoph Rilke

Letters to a Young Poet

The Notebooks of Malte Laurids Brigge

The Selected Poetry of Rainer Maria Rilke

The Frog Prince

THE
FROG PRINCE

A Fairy Tale for
Consenting Adults

STEPHEN MITCHELL

HARMONY BOOKS · NEW YORK

The passages quoted on pp. 22f., 70, 126, 145, and 170 are reprinted from *Tao Te Ching: A New English Version* by Stephen Mitchell, HarperCollins, 1988.

Published by Harmony Books, 201 East 50th Street, New York, New York 10022. Member of the Crown Publishing Group. Random House, Inc. New York, Toronto, London, Sydney, Auckland
www.randomhouse.com

Harmony Books is a registered trademark and Harmony Books colophon is a trademark of Random House, Inc.
Printed in the United States of America

Design by Barbara Balch

Library of Congress Cataloging-in-Publication Data

Mitchell, Stephen, 1943–
The frog prince : a fairy tale for consenting adults / by Stephen Mitchell.—1st ed.
    I. Fiction.   2. Fairy tales—Adaptations.   I. Title.
        PS3563.I8235F76   1999
        813'.54—dc21   99-20433

ISBN 0-609-60545-3

10 9 8 7 6 5 4 3 2 1

First Edition

To Vicki

Imaginary gardens with real toads in them . . .

MARIANNE MOORE

The Frog Prince

I

Princes and Frogs

There are two kinds of women: those who marry princes and those who marry frogs. The frogs never become princes, but it is an acknowledged fact that a prince may very well, in the course of an ordinary marriage, gradually, at first almost imperceptibly, turn into a frog. Happy the woman who after twenty-five years still wakes up beside the prince she fell in love with.

Entropy is the name that our scientists give to this phenomenon, the irreversible downward slide of events: life becomes death, order becomes disorder, princes become frogs. That is the way of the world, scientists say, and most of us solemnly nod our heads in agreement. But the rules of physics, though they resemble the rules of an ordinary marriage, do not at all correspond to the rules of the human soul. There are no exceptions to the rules of physics, whereas the rules of the soul consist of nothing *but* exceptions. That is why I want to tell you a different kind of love story, about a frog who became a prince.

II

Once Upon a Time

It all began . . .

But let me step back and begin before the actual beginning. There is a good deal of background material that I ought to fill you in on, and a certain number of necessary explanations. The traditional rendition of the story, which we can call the Condensed Version, tells everything in six and a half minutes, plunging straight into the thick of things with the Princess and her golden ball. Besides, it is a version for children, who don't require explanations of the extraordinary. Children understand that *Once upon a time* refers not only—not even primarily—to the past, but to the impalpable regions of the present, the deeper places inside us, where princes and dragons, wizards and talking birds, impassable roads, impossible tasks, and happy endings have always existed, alive and bursting with psychic power.

Let me start by reminding you that not all princesses in these ancient tales are beautiful. They don't *have* to be: they are princesses. But our princess was, in fact, a most attractive young woman. How attractive? Well, the Condensed Version, which is usually quite straightforward about details, gets caught up in its enthusiasm when it describes her. "She was so beautiful," it says, "that the sun, who had seen so many things, was filled with wonder every time he shined onto her face." This is charming, to be sure, but why the hyperbole? It is true that the Princess was lovely; you might even have called her—on certain days, in certain moods, in certain rare subtleties of light—beautiful. But there are many beautiful young women scattered across the globe, walking in high heels or in sneakers down every main street of every city on earth, and if the sun were to stop and stare at each of them, our days and our nights would be longer than I can easily tell. No, exaggerations like this don't occur to a storyteller out of the blue; there is always a reason, and the reason here, I think, is that the more difficult side of our princess's character must have made the teller of the Condensed Version uncomfortable. For the outer mirrors the inner, and there is no character flaw that, to a discerning eye, does not manifest itself on the faces of even the surpassingly beautiful, making them far less a cause for wonder than is the face of a plain young woman with a loving heart.

In short, the Princess was proud; she was ungrateful; she was headstrong. But we will come to all that in due course.

Our story takes place in the High Renaissance,

in one of the small, prosperous French kingdoms whose châteaux along the Loire and the Saône are among the glories of European architecture. "French kingdoms, plural?" you may be asking. It is a natural question, and I must stop again to explain.

III

The Crack on the Surface of Reality

$\mathcal{A}$ century and three quarters before our story begins, during the first, tentative stages of the Renaissance, when one Western mind-world was dying and another was in the throes of being born, the wisest men and women in Europe could observe a hairline crack, as it were, on the surface of reality. This kind of crack is more likely to form in the life of an individual than in the life of an entire culture. When a woman or a man undergoes a deep spiritual transformation, there are certain critical points along the way when what is partial needs to be shattered in order to become what is whole. At such points, the hidden powers and illnesses of the soul may be unleashed, giving rise to bizarre phenomena in which darkness and light are interchangeable and in which it is sometimes difficult to distinguish miracle from madness.

That is what was happening in Europe during the early years of the Renaissance, and why the wise women and men of the time were so deeply concerned. Travelers had begun to sight giants in the mountains and forests. Wish-bestowing rings were appearing suddenly on the dusty back shelves of jewelry shops in small provincial towns. Farmers' sons would plant a bean, and it was a toss-up whether an ordinary beanstalk would grow in its place or a beanstalk whose top punctured the clouds. Fishermen would reel in their catch, and sometimes a fish would silently thrash about in its death-agony as fish had always done, and sometimes it would stand up on its tail and, in a suave baritone that might have been coming from the mouth of a character in a Noël Coward play, offer the fisherman three gifts in return for its freedom. Hunters would be riding in pursuit of a deer or a fox, and suddenly the deer or fox would halt, wheel about, and address them in perfect High German or in a French so elegant that a committee of scholars from the Sorbonne would not only have approved but applauded. Articulate animals were, in fact, popping up all over the place: talking deer, foxes, frogs, flounders, hares, hedgehogs, salamanders, goats, geese, mice, rats, cats, dogs of every breed, nightingales, sparrows, owls, hawks, wolves, horses (whole horses or, on one occasion, just a severed head), donkeys, lions, bears, and assorted other large, hitherto-silent carnivores. Magic was afoot everywhere. Things were getting out of hand.

Now, it is perfectly fine for a deer or fox, in a dream or on one of the other borderlands of reality, to give us a well-timed piece of advice once in a great while. But when what happens inside the soul spills up into our outer, physical world, life can become extremely difficult, and sometimes extremely frightening. And when *Once upon a time* erupts across an entire culture, things can get very dicey indeed. In such a crisis, we need all the wisdom we can find.

That is why, after the crack on the surface of reality had been noticed and observed for several years, a delegation of wise men and women went to the King of France and the King of Germany to request—to insist—that their respective governments be decentralized, at least until after this crisis had passed. Wielding political power, they said (quoting the Tao Te Ching, which had been brought back to Europe by Marco Polo a hundred years earlier, at the beginning of the fourteenth century), incurs grave responsibilities and, as with spiritual power, many a good man has wandered off the path and become deeply entangled in the brambles of personal ambition or shortsighted ideals. The truth about power, they said, is that the more you are given, the deeper is your obligation to let go of it. The wise ruler does his job and then steps back: he understands that the universe is forever out of control and that trying to dominate events goes against the current of the Tao; he lets things go their own way and resides at the center of the circle, they said.

The King of France and the King of Germany were reasonable men. Whether they agreed to the decentralization *because* they were reasonable men or because the uncanniness of events had frightened them to the tips of their royal toes, no one knew. The fact is, however, that they did agree, and in the aftermath of their decision, several dozen independent kingdoms sprang up throughout Germany and France. This was still the situation 175 years later, at the end of the sixteenth century, when our story takes place. (Two subsequent delegations were dispatched, whose job was to nourish the growth of spiritual sanity in Europe and to make a report on the frequency of Unusual Phenomena. The second delegation, which included Rabelais, Erasmus, and the young Louise

Labé, met in 1536, as the time of the giants was drawing to an end; and the final delegation, the one that abolished independent kingdoms in France, met in 1606, just after the publication of the first part of *Don Quixote,* when the crack on the surface of reality had painfully but mercifully closed.)

IV

Life at Court

Our particular royal court was nestled in one of the loveliest regions of France, a valley in which the river Loire winds its languid cerulean S through orchards, meadows, and fields whose lushness of color is equaled only by the luxuriance of their fertility. France is the capital of beauty, and I will have to be careful in this chapter not to get seduced into the purpler regions of English prose.

Life at court was very pleasant. The King and Queen spent their days administering their estates, cultivating the arts, and caring for the poor. The palace was a house where all was accustomed, ceremonious, with a custom not dulled, but enhanced, by repetition: the courtiers moved in the stately, fluid motions inculcated by the pavanes, galliards, and other court dances of the time; the air was filled with the sweet sound of music, provided by a full orchestra, a chamber orchestra, and three separate string trios, all of which constituted less than half of the music entry on the royal payroll; everyone enjoyed the daily rituals in which even the lowest-ranking footman had the dignity of an appointed role—the formal *levées* and *couchées*, the great state dinners, the poetry readings, the moonlit suppers on the grass at which the ladies' rustling silks and satins were echoed by the rustling of the leaves; everyone treasured the freedom of a court that allowed the King's fool to be as barbed and witty as he pleased without fear of a whipping, and the ministers of state to be so in love with the panache of their burgeoning language that sometimes in the midst of a policy speech, enraptured, they would burst into the French equivalent of blank verse. Outside the court, life was almost as pleasant: harvests were plentiful; holidays were frequent, with free food and drink served to the peasantry on the royal picnic grounds along the banks of the river; and it should come as no surprise that even the language of the poor was rich in words that made subtle distinctions between varieties of happiness, words such as *blithe, gleeful, mirthful, jocund, merry,* and *jolly,* which in the English of our solemn century have withered from disuse. In fact, the only shadow cast on the perfect well-being of the kingdom was the anxiety that people felt about Unusual Phenomena, although, to everyone's relief, these had been gradually decreasing until they now averaged only two or three per country per decade. The latest incident (it involved a magic bird and a wicked stepmother who had killed her little stepson, cooked his diced flesh into a stew, and served it to his unwitting father) had occured five years before our story begins, in a village near the King's favorite hunting lodge, and was particularly troubling, even though it did end happily.

The King, the Queen, the ministers, the courtiers, even the footmen and the Fool, were true Renaissance men and women, each of them skilled in many modes of human activity, and each would be worthy of our attention. But since all the characters in this story, with the exception of the Princess and the Frog, play no more than supporting roles, it is hardly necessary to describe the intricacies of their lives or to fill you in on their backgrounds: what triumphs and defeats during his long reign had shaped the King into the exemplar of a wise monarch, or why the Queen had ended up insisting that each of the palace's eighty-seven rooms be decorated in a different shade of purple. There is, after all, only a finite quantity of time to be spent in telling a story, and although it is true that all individual things are interconnected in one vast web of being, so that—because any strand can eventually be followed through the space-time fabric of the entire universe—one could at this point easily shift into the history of wisdom in China or of beauty in France, the origin of species or the origin of reality, the Tao of leadership, the topology of the soul, or the esoteric symbolism of colors, it is equally true that one needs to arrive at the beginning of a story before one can tell it.

Once upon a time, then, there was a princess. . . .

V

At the Well

The Princess has walked into the forest on a cool May afternoon and is sitting on the stone rim of the well. She is dressed casually—for a princess—in one of her favorite walking outfits: a wide-sleeved low-necked short-ruffed fuchsia velvet bodice covering an eggshell-colored silk chemise, and a long forest-green velvet skirt over three stiff petticoats (no farthingale). Her long black hair, uncapped today and unpowdered, hangs down almost to her waist, as loosely as a bride's. She is wearing no makeup but a touch of eyeliner around her dark brown eyes and a dab of blush on her alabaster cheeks, no jewelry but a pair of small gold earrings and her second-best crown, of a thread-thin gold filigree so tactful that you would barely notice it. In her right hand she is holding her golden ball, which seems as bright and beautiful as her own independence. She gazes past the distorted reflection of her face, into its depths.

Since the Princess is earlier than usual, the Frog has not yet surfaced to see if she has come. The Frog sits in the mud at the bottom of the well, breathing through his skin. His nostrils are closed. He is in deep meditation. The water feels cold but comfortable. There is a small eddy near the surface; or is it near the surface of his mind? He sits motionless, silent except for an occasional, inconsequential croak.

Neither the Frog nor the Princess has any inkling of how utterly their lives are about to change.

We are now poised on the brink of events, the fulcrum of the story: the fulcrum of the universe.

And what a pleasure it is to be here! How I love the beginnings of things: the first glint of dawn, the blank page, the vastness in an infant's eyes, all those shimmering moments when life is filled with pure possibility, and one would do anything—almost anything—to prolong the wonder of it. *Verweile doch, du bist so schön!* "O moment, you are so beautiful, stay with me a while longer," as Faust said in another context.

But the Princess is about to lose hold of her golden ball, and our story as a result is about to roll over the edge of becoming. This is the crucial moment.

All right. Let us stop now and focus our attention on the Princess's right hand. Up to this moment, she has been holding the golden ball, as she contemplates it, in the middle of her palm, with a grip neither too loose nor too firm. Her hand has been alert all through its nerves and fibers, alive with awareness, a concentration of her entire body. Up to this moment. And now, suddenly, the hand forgets itself. It grows limp. Its fingers uncurl. The golden ball totters, rolls half an inch backward, half an inch forward, pauses for an instant, then rolls down the ramp of her three middle fingers, over the edge of the fingertips, through two feet of air and into the well, with a loud, peremptory splash.

How could this have happened?

A star falls through the sky and we make a wish. To us it seems that the star is falling. But to the inhabitants of the star, the star is going neither down nor up but is stationary in a sky that proceeds along its ordinary course on a day like any other. Up and down are, after all, relative in the world of physics, and in the world of the soul they are often one and the same. What we are tempted to call a disaster is sometimes the first, painful stage of a blessing.

A rare and gifted person at the height of a soul-crisis can see that there is an intelligence that shapes our ends, rough-hew them as we will. And though on ordinary days we may persist in clinging to our own agendas, though we may think we know what is good for us and keep trying to make it happen, what we want is not necessarily what we deeply need. Some presence inside us knows better. That presence is the author of apparent disasters.

This can be stated from a slightly different perspective: Character is fate. Even though we are passionately attached, as personalities, to the stasis of our ordinary discontents, sometimes the critical moment arrives when on a deeper level we are ready for the world to fall apart. At such moments a disaster is precisely what we (unconsciously) long for.

The Princess comes to herself. A brief fibrillation thrills through the nerves of her empty hand. She sees the splash. She bursts into sobs.

VI

The Frog in Love

The Frog, as I have told you, was sitting at the bottom of the well. What I have not yet told you is that he was in love.

This was a very meditative frog. Ever since he could remember, he had spent most of his life simply observing his breath as he sat in the high grass or under the old linden tree or in the mud at the bottom of the well. There were forays from time to time, of course, when he would surface to catch a few dozen flies with a tongue that shot out and back from the floor of his mouth like a long, flexible, sticky-pointed arrow. One did have to live, after all, and although he took no pleasure in killing, he was an animal among animals. But however necessary his hunting expeditions were, they seemed like diversions. He much preferred to be watching his breath, diving deep through the waters of his own serenity.

Three months before the beginning of our story, this almost uninterrupted calm had been . . . *shattered* is too violent a word, and inaccurate besides. It is not as if his calm were a plate-glass window through which life had thrown a large rock. No, let us say *roiled*. His calm had been roiled. There was now a continual source of agitation, excitement, and longing in the waters of his mind. He had seen the Princess.

Why this hadn't happened before, we can only guess. The Princess had been coming to the well for many years. The Frog had lived there for as long as he could remember. It is true that he usually emerged at night, but there was many an afternoon hour that he spent sitting in meditation on the well's rim or under the linden tree, motionless except for the occasional flick of his tongue. Had she never come there except when he was underwater? Or had he always been so absorbed that he simply hadn't noticed her?

He did notice her this time. It felt as if a bolt of energy had flashed through his eyes and electrified his whole body. It was a physical sensation, but the shock itself was not physical. It was a shock of understanding. He knew, beyond a doubt, that he and the Princess were meant for each other.

This had nothing to do with the fact that she was beautiful. Many things were beautiful. Light was beautiful, and mud, and the tall bending grass, and the sky on a cloudy day, and the quick green-and-gold flies that buzzed through his sleepy gaze on a summer afternoon, and the shadowed underside of a leaf on the surface of the well, and water itself: water was perhaps the most beautiful thing of all. It was not her beauty that touched him so deeply. It was something else in her, or perhaps it was not in her but in the electrified space between them. Whatever that something was, it made him want to draw closer to her. A frog and a woman? A frog and a *princess* no less? He realized how unnatural this desire to be near her was. He didn't know how to approach her. But somehow, he knew, they would be together, they *had* to be together, in an intimacy that was deeper than he had ever dived.

During the next three months, the Frog spent many hours meditating on what it meant to be so completely, so absurdly, in love. And many, many hours watching the Princess as she sat by the well: an unobserved observer: two large eyes dark with longing that poked through the water like two periscopes.

VII

The View from the Bottom

The Frog was sitting in a state of deep meditation at the bottom of the well.

Later on, when he had time to consider the events of the day, he recalled the splash as if it had been simultaneously etched, with silver-point clarity, onto each of his senses. The moment had been complete in itself, an exquisite little poem:

> Old well,
>> thing falls in—
>>> the sound of the water.

Only that sound in the whole universe.

At first, of course, he had no idea that the "thing" was a golden ball. Startled, he looked up. Something had plunged through the roiling, sunlight-skimmed surface of the well: a vague form much larger than a fly, but how large he couldn't tell in all the watery commotion. An instant later he could see a glint, a curve: it was round, this thing; it was bright, it was sinking through the seethe of waves and bubbles; it was gold, it was spherical; it was a golden ball; it was the *Princess's* golden ball plummeting through the stirred-up water straight toward him. He blinked and leapt. The ball half-buried itself in the mud.

Once the mud-clouds had begun to settle, the Frog glanced at the ball, which had become embedded in such a way that its seam was visible, along with its small golden clasp. Then a new sound drew his attention upward. Someone was sobbing.

But I am moving too fast now, having started to think in human time again. Ranic time is much slower, and the moments that we are barely conscious of as they whiz by are, for a frog, packed with experience. It is like . . . What's that pitcher's name? You know: the one in the late sixties who pitched a perfect game while he was on LSD. He later said that his awareness had expanded so much that each moment felt endless, and he could wind up and throw in an infinite slow-motion, as if he had all the time in the universe.

The Frog knew that the sobbing was human. He had never heard anyone sob before. The sounds of the forest that he knew so well came from creatures unacquainted with grief. The nearest analogy was the howling of wolves, yet that sound was not the voice of sorrow but of a solitude bursting free and exulting in the joy of its own expression. No, he had heard nothing like this human cry.

As he listened, he could feel himself opening and turning toward the sorrow, as a flower turns toward the sunlight. He felt moved to the depths of his animal heart. Not overwhelmed: the grief did not belong to him. But somehow he could hold it, move into it, recognize it as a season of his inner landscape, when the water becomes very cold and your respiration slows to almost nothing and life creeps along at an infinitesimal pace because that is the only way you can endure.

The Frog was not yet aware that the sobbing came from a woman. This is important to notice. The sequence was not that he first recognized the Princess's voice and only then, being in love with her, was he moved. This personal sympathy, though admirable in a frog and indeed in a human being, would have been a more limited mode of compassion than the spontaneous, undifferentiated, pure compassion which, in fact, arose before he ever recognized the Princess's voice.

As his heart quivered in response, his feet kicked off from the bottom of the well. Perhaps there was some way he could help.

VIII

Enter the Frog

The Frog is now treading water on the surface of the well. He sees the Princess. His eyes are dark with love. His heart quivers. He opens his mouth to speak.

Here is how the Condensed Version reports the event: "And as she sobbed, someone called to her, 'What is the matter, dear Princess? Your sobbing would move a stone to compassion.' She looked around to see where the voice was coming from, and what she saw was a frog, sticking his thick ugly head out of the water."

Is this account accurate? Yes. Does it quote

the Frog's speech verbatim? Yes. Was the Princess's first reaction really one of disgust? Well, yes and no.

This was obviously not an instance of love at first sight. The Princess had an acutely developed sense of beauty, even for a Frenchwoman, and was correspondingly sensitive to its opposite. She shrunk from ugliness; it pained her almost physically; it entered her eyes the way a nasty odor enters your nose. And in her defense, it must be confessed that frogs, those "amphibious dwarfs" (in the words of a modern French poet), with their bulging eyes and neckless heads and stunted arms and fat clammy white bellies, cannot properly be classed with gazelles or cats as paragons of loveliness in the animal realm. Nor did she have much experience of them. She had occasionally glimpsed one hopping through the grass as she walked in the forest or sat beside the well (it was never *our* frog), but the only aspect of them that she knew well was their legs, sautéed in butter and garlic, lightly seasoned with pepper, and served before her on a

golden plate several times a week, at the chef's discretion, as a second or third hors d'œuvre.

So yes: she did at first shrink from the Frog
with a physical revulsion. At the same time, she was
intrigued. She had never personally encountered
a talking animal, though she had heard all the
stories and had attended the councils of state con-
vened to discuss the problem of Unusual Phenomena. But whereas her parents and the rest of
the kingdom dreaded the prospect of a new incident breaking out, she felt her interest piqued.
She had even, on occasion, musing at the edge of
the well, tried to imagine what she would say if a
huge sixteen-pointed stag addressed her, or an
eagle with smoldering eyes.

But there was still another emotion that arose
in her along with the disgust and the curiosity, an
emotion that was even stronger than the other two,
though she was not aware of it at the time, and
indeed not until she recollected the incident
much later did she realize how strong that emotion
had been. It is important to understand that she

was, for the first time in her adult life, in a state of intense vulnerability. She was feeling grief-stricken, she had had her sobbing suddenly interrupted by a vision of ugliness, had found herself tête-à-tête with an animal speaking the language of Ronsard and du Bellay in the purest Touraine accent. It was not precisely the sound of his voice—midway between a high baritone and a low tenor—that touched her so deeply, but something that radiated through the sound: a quality of kindness. She was used to being admired, adored. To be looked at through empathetic frog eyes was a startling experience.

In the swirl of the Princess's emotions, grief was still uppermost, and an inarticulate mourning for her lost independence. But deeper down, beneath the level of consciousness, in the dark and fertile soil of her heart, love had planted itself like a mustard seed.

IX

The Offer

"Oh, Frog," the Princess said, sniffling, "it is sweet of you to ask. But you wouldn't understand."

"Perhaps not," said the Frog in his gentle, melodious voice. "But perhaps I can help, even so."

"If only you could," the Princess said. "Things look so bleak." She sniffled again and wiped her eyes. Little smears of eyeliner appeared on the back of her wrist.

"Wait just a minute," the Frog said. He climbed out of the water, jumped onto the grass, hopped over to a large maple tree, picked up a leaf with his mouth, hopped to the well, and jumped back onto its stone rim. "Mhere," he said, holding out the leaf to her. "Mlow your mose im mis. I will glose my eyes."

It was a large maple leaf that had just begun to lose its moisture, and it would indeed have served as a rude substitute for a handkerchief had the Princess forgotten hers. She smiled, touched by the gesture.

"Thank you, Frog," she said. "I have something better, but thank you just the same. And please do close your eyes." She took an embroidered handkerchief of fine cambric out of her purse, dried her tears, and blew her nose as delicately as she could. "There. You may open your eyes."

The Frog blinked. "How are you feeling now, Your Highness?"

"Oh, a very little bit better. But not much. And you needn't address me as 'Your Highness,' you know. We are not at court. We are in the forest."

"As you wish, Your . . . ," said the Frog. There was a brief silence. "And if you feel like telling me what has made you so sad, I would be glad to listen, even though I may not understand." He was sitting a foot away from the Princess, his head tilted slightly, looking up at her with an expression of deep concern.

"What good would that do?" the Princess said. "How can you possibly help?" A single tear welled up in the corner of her left eye, sparkled there for an instant, then rolled onto her cheek.

"I really don't know," said the Frog. "But I know that I would *like* to help. Why don't you tell me and see?"

"You wouldn't by any chance be magic, would you?" the Princess said, her face brightening. "Have you brought me something? Three wishes, perhaps?"

"Alas, no. I am not that kind of animal. I have brought you only myself."

"Not even *one* wish?"

"Not even one."

"Oh well," the Princess said, with a sigh. "I suppose I will never see my golden ball again."

"Your golden ball?"

"Yes. I dropped my golden ball into the well. It was very clumsy of me. I don't know how it happened." This last sentence and the memory of the splash almost caused the Princess to break into sobs again. Only with the greatest effort did she manage to control herself.

"I have seen your ball," the Frog said, a bit disingenuously. "It is beautiful. But can't you buy another one, or can't His Majesty your father have another one made for you?"

"It wouldn't be the same. I have held my golden ball so close. I feel as if I have lost part of myself."

"Does it mean that much to you?"

"It means my freedom. It means everything."

"I am so sorry. And nothing can replace it?"

"Nothing."

"In that case," said the Frog, "I will find it. I will bring it back for you."

The Princess was silent. There was an abstracted look in her eyes.

"Princess. Princess, did you hear me?"

The Princess turned to him with a wan smile. "Forgive me," she said, "I wasn't paying attention. Did you say something?"

"I said that I would bring back your golden ball."

"That is very nice."

"It is true! I will do it! I would do anything for you. I love you."

For a moment the Princess was speechless with surprise. Then she burst out laughing. Her vivid, silvery laughter echoed through the forest.

The Frog looked down into the well. He saw a frog's face staring back at him. It was thick and ugly, and sad.

X

The Test of the Three Balls

$\mathcal{B}$ut why, you may be wondering, was the golden ball of such grave importance to the Princess? What made her think that she had lost her freedom? To understand, you need to know a little about her upbringing.

A modern princess—of England, say, or Monaco—serves the purpose of being an adornment in the fantasy life of the public. Consequently, she receives the kind of education that one might think of giving to a particularly splendid papier-mâché angel before putting it at the top of the Christmas tree: an education whose main goal is proficiency in the arts of looking pretty and standing straight. Our century, whatever virtues it may have, is not an optimal time for princesses.

Things were different in the Renaissance. Intelligence had a primary value then. At almost every level of the social order, education was meant to create true amateurs—people who were in love with quality. A gentleman or a lady needed to be at least minimally skilled in many arts, because that was considered the fittest way of appreciating the good things in life and honoring the goodness of life itself. Nor did being well-rounded mean smoothing over your finest points and becoming like the reflection of a smile in a polished teaspoon. Intelligence walked hand in hand with individuality, although having finely sharpened points of view did not, it was felt, require you to poke other people with them. If wit was a rapier, courtesy was the button at the end of the blade.

The Princess had been trained by some of the greatest scholars in France. By the time she was twenty-one, she had become proficient in the arts of poetry, mathematics, history, philosophy, architecture, rhetoric, singing, dancing, riding, drawing, archery, astronomy, eloquence, and disappointment. She spoke fluent Italian, Spanish, German, and Chinese, elegant Latin (though her style was perhaps a shade too Ciceronian), and her Greek was so flawless that a repartee in that language had once stopped the mouth of a smug, Aristotle-quoting ambassador from the Duke of Athens.

The King and the Queen were immensely proud of their daughter's reputation as one of the most accomplished princesses in Europe. The only thing that worried them was her growing independence, which took the form of an intense love of solitude. As she got older, she found that she was less and less able to participate in the constant merriment of court life. With polite but firm excuses, she would absent herself from some court function—a play or a speech or a flower-viewing excursion—and would walk or ride off by herself, sometimes stopping to spend the whole afternoon in her secret spot by the abandoned well, in the forest to the east of the palace. The more the King reminded her of her political duties, the more she would quote back to him a favorite passage from Chuang-tzu that he had first taught her when she was a carefree little girl of nine:

As Chuang-tzu was fishing in the river Pu, two messengers came from the King of Chu and said, "The King requests that you come to the capital and serve as his prime minister." Chuang-tzu said, "I have heard that in Chu there is a sacred tortoise that died three thousand years ago. The King keeps its shell in the holiest of his temples, wrapped in silk and encased in a golden box. Now, if you were the tortoise, would you prefer to be venerated in such a way or would you rather be alive again, crawling around in the mud?" The messengers said, "The latter, certainly." Chuang-tzu said, "Give my compliments to His Majesty, and tell him that I am happy right here, crawling around in the mud."

The Princess would tell her father, politely yet firmly, that she didn't believe she had any obligation at all to prepare herself for ruling his kingdom, or any other kingdom, for that matter. She didn't yet know what she wanted to do with her life, she would say, but to make laws and administer estates, to reward good deeds and punish bad ones, seemed to her a dreary, unimaginative way of spending one's time and energy. As for the constant esthetic whirl at court, the admiration of those in whose interest it was to admire her, the public display of her talents in a society where she was necessarily the glass of fashion and the mold of form, the observed of all observers—there were moments when this life felt so insipid to her that she would gladly have changed places (at least for an hour or so) with the filthiest, most ungrammatical groom in the royal stables.

Nor did the Princess set much store by what is now known as romantic love. She had seen too much of it and its sad aftermath among the ladies and gentlemen of the nobility to believe in its value as a compass in the uncharted territory of human happiness. It began, she knew from the tales of her ladies-in-waiting, with a catch in the breath and a tickling in the groin; continued with sighs, smiles, fluttering eyelashes, moonings, croonings, crumpled notes, Petrarchan sonnets, assignations in the shrubbery, idealizations that made Plato seem like the veriest grocer, and the self-absorption of gratified desire; and ended when the stark light of reality dawned. Time and again she had seen romantic love run its course from intoxication to misery. This was not the path to peace of heart. It would be much wiser, she thought, to entrust her happiness to chance. Not to chance pure and simple, of course, but to chance refined by a modicum of prudent psychological engineering.

So it happened that when the Princess reached the age of sixteen and the King and Queen insisted that she receive at least one per year of the many suitors who were begging for her hand in marriage, she devised the Test of the Three Balls.

The rules were simple. A suitor was required, first of all, to take a solemn vow never to breathe a word, even to his dearest friend, about the proceedings. If he passed the Test, she would consent to marry him. If he failed, however, he had to renounce the company of women for the following three years.

This proviso succeeded in somewhat thinning out the long list of kings, princes, dukes, marquesses, and counts who were eager to claim her.

But there were many left, from every corner of France.

Nor could the Test itself have been more simple. A suitor would enter the Princess's reception hall and would be conducted by one of her ladies-in-waiting to a long mahogany table. There, in a horizontal line, he would find three hinged and hollow metal balls, each four inches in diameter: a golden ball, a silver ball, and a leaden ball. One of them, he would be told, enclosed the Princess's portrait (an enchantingly lifelike miniature by Caravaggio); the other two enclosed nothing but empty air. He would then be given three minutes to make his choice.

The Princess always enjoyed these three-minute ordeals. If the Test had been taking place anywhere else in Europe, she realized, she could not have been so certain of the outcome. She might have had to worry that one of the dashing noblemen would choose the golden ball, her talisman, her seal of independence—and thereby condemn her, once the haze of romantic love had lifted, to a life of obligations and boredom. But this was France. This was, throughout all its kingdoms, the land of intellectual subtlety. No intelligent, self-respecting prince would ever choose the simplest solution, especially since she herself, the deviser of the Test, was known as the most intimidatingly astute of princesses. She could see the thought process unfold on their faces, always the same, as if inscribed in actual words on their handsome, wrinkled brows. *So may the outward shows be least themselves . . . ,* they would ponder; *there is no vice so simple but assumes some mark of virtue on its outward parts. . . . It is like this in law, in war, in beauty. . . .* And then, as the apparent solution was revealed: *Therefore I will refuse this gaudy gold, nor shall this simpering silver draw me to it; but you, O modest, barely-shining lead, whose plainness moves me more than eloquence: you I will choose, and with you cast my lot.* A dependable lot, thank goodness. She would have to suppress a smile, every time, at how unthinkable, to a cultivated French mind, the obvious choice was. Poor fellows: if she weren't so pleased to be assured of another whole year of freedom, she might be tempted to pity them as the leaden ball swung open on its hinges to reveal . . . not her portrait . . . no: nothing but empty air.

XI

Looking Down, Looking Up

We are at the well. The Frog is still looking at his reflection in the water. The Princess, though she is still laughing, is sad. The Frog is sad. The Princess feels hopeless. The Frog feels humiliated. Inaction threatens overhead, like the distant rumble of thunder. This is a moment when with the least bit less love on the Frog's part, or the least bit more discouragement, the story would unravel: In a parallel universe of stories, a parallel Frog jumps back into the well, a parallel Princess trudges home to the palace, the law of the irreconcilable differences of opposites clicks into effect, the world-snake slithers off into the grass and never makes the necessary turn that allows it to swallow its own tail.

At moments like this, character is decisive. It is not a question of victory or defeat, but of surrender to one's sense of what must be.

It is also, from another perspective, a question of one's relation to mirrors. Narcissism is a temptation not only for the beautiful but for the ugly as well. Desire and aversion are, after all, reverse sides of the same coin, and Narcissus and Anti-Narcissus were twins: Narcissus who, bending over the pool, fell in love with his own image; Anti-Narcissus who ran away, repulsed by his image, and lost the chance to keep looking until he could see through it, into the life of the pool itself.

The Frog stares at the face staring back at him. For the first time in his life he knows that he is ugly. This, as a fact in itself, does not trouble him so very much. True, he was born and bred in France, but French animals are more animal than French. What does trouble him is the realization that the Princess finds him repulsive. However remote the possibility that the Princess might someday love him has been up to now, it has still been a possibility. Now it seems . . . ugh, worse than hopeless. Oh, she may come to love him as a pet, or even, if he is very lucky, as a friend. But never will she love him truly, intimately, as a lover. He knows what her look meant. There is not the slightest ghost of a chance.

He is desolate. He is mortified. His heart aches. He feels a strong tug toward the water. Perhaps it is time now to bow out as gracefully as he can and plunge into his proper element, the mud at the bottom of the well.

Thirteen seconds have gone by since the Princess began to laugh. Her high, silvery laughter echoes through the tops of the trees.

The Frog looks up. In staring at his own face, he has forgotten the Princess's. She is as beautiful in mirth as in sorrow. But it is not her beauty that touches him so deeply, it is . . . And, to his great astonishment, the Frog feels something in the space between them: that same quality he felt so long ago. Nothing has changed. Yes, it is impossible for her to love him: *that* he can't deny. Yet he knows, absurdly, beyond a doubt, that he and the Princess are meant for each other. Somehow, by some miracle, some twist in the way things are, they will be together. He can swallow his humiliation like a foul-tasting insect. He can bide his time. He can bring the Princess her golden ball, and then perhaps she will begin to love him. Or like him. Or at least not laugh at him.

XII

Wishes

"I am sorry, Frog," the Princess said after she had stopped laughing and had given her eyes a few dabs with a clean corner of her handkerchief. "I hope I didn't hurt your feelings."

"Well, Your Highness, I must confess that my heart does feel a little bruised."

"Poor Frog," the Princess said. She looked into his eyes. He looked into her eyes.

"On the other hand," said the Frog, "it is a pleasure to see your sorrow lift, even for a little while. At least I have brought you a few moments of happiness."

"Well, yes," the Princess said, with a sigh.

"I may be ridiculous as a suitor, but I am a good jester, though I didn't mean to be."

"No, of course you weren't jesting. I am sure that you love me. So many men do. But I have never been loved by a frog before. I didn't mean to be rude."

"That is all right. It isn't your fault. I can't ease my own pain, but I can still try to ease yours."

"Oh, Frog, that is very generous of you."

"Why should we both be sad?"

"Why indeed?"

"I will bring you your golden ball. And if something is to be, it will be."

"Yes," said the Princess, who two years before had written, for her philosophy tutor, an excellent essay on fate and free will, demonstrating that the very terms of the problem are delusory and that the only primary freedom is freedom from our

own ideas. "I would owe you a great debt of gratitude. Almost as much as if you had brought me
three wishes. Of course, I would have wished for
that first."

"To have your golden ball?"

"My beautiful golden ball. Yes, that would have
been my first wish."

"And what else would you have wished for?"

"Why do you wish to know?"

"Oh, I am just curious. I would like to know *you*
a little better."

"Well, I don't mind telling you. As long as you
agree to tell me something in return."

"All right. That seems fair."

"Now then, my second wish . . . My second wish
would be . . ."

"You know, of course," the Frog said, "that you
are not allowed to wish for world peace or the end
of poverty."

"Why is that? Not that I would necessarily sac-
rifice my last two wishes."

"I don't know. Wishes just don't work that way, it seems. I have a friend, a fox, who is an expert in these matters. He says that wishes are like magnifying glasses: they enlarge and focus an intention that is already inside us."

"Ah. Well, let me think."

"Take as much time as you want."

"I will give myself three minutes," said the Princess, who, being a quick-witted and decisive young woman, found that three minutes were more than enough.

"Here is what I would wish, Frog. My second wish would be for a prince who loves me with all his heart, a prince who is a real person and not some bright, charming nitwit. And thirdly I would wish not to be rich and famous."

"Really!" said the Frog, his heart swelling with admiration and despair.

"Yes. I would wish to live a life of *solitude à deux,* in a small cottage in the forest, with a good library and a lute and a telescope and a gardener and a dozen servants. Perhaps a cook as well. I am not very interested in cooking."

"It couldn't be *too* small a cottage then."

"No, I wouldn't wish to be poor. I would be somewhere in the middle. 'The simplest pattern is the clearest.'"

"The Tao Te Ching?"

"Of course."

"Well, that sounds very nice. A cottage in the forest, and a handsome prince."

"Now *you* tell *me* something," said the Princess. "How did you become a frog?"

"How did I *become* a frog?"

"Yes. What happened?"

"I don't know that *any*thing happened. I was a tadpole. Then I grew up and was—am—a frog."

"But *some*thing must have happened. How did you come to speak? Most frogs don't, you know."

"Is that so? I am afraid I don't know any other frogs. I do know a fox, as I said. Our conversations are telepathic. All I can tell you is that you came and I spoke. I had never spoken before. I had never needed to."

"Well, this makes no sense if you are just a frog. Frogs don't wake up one fine morning and decide to speak, just like that."

"But I didn't decide a thing. You were crying. I wanted to help. I saw you and opened my mouth. The words came out by themselves."

"You may say what you like," the Princess said, folding her arms across her chest. "You may remember what you like. But nothing you can possibly say will persuade me that you are not really a prince."

The Frog could see that she was a very determined young woman.

XIII

Not All Talking Frogs Are Enchanted Princes

Who was the Frog, really?

The Condensed Version is unambiguous: it says, without any qualification, that the Frog (or rather, the former and future Prince) had been put under an enchantment by a wicked witch. As to how this had happened, what had been the cause of the witch's malice, and why the Prince had been vulnerable to the spell—it passes over such details in silence. But the truth of the matter is more obscure than this tidy explanation implies, and while tidiness is often a virtue in storytelling, the lack of certainty about who our particular frog had been is one of the most important elements in the story.

The fact is that not all talking frogs are enchanted princes. A talking frog may be simply a talking frog: conscious, sensitive, articulate, yet with no human past, and no future in any form but its own moist, amphibious body.

Was our frog a prince? This was a question that would never have occurred to him. His memory reached back to his earliest days in and around the well but no further than that. There had been two particular moments, it is true, when he had felt a dim recollection of having been something different, something more: his mind had been filled— once by the scent of jasmine on a spring morning, once by the fall of a maple leaf—with scenes (remembered? imagined?) that were tall and dry and strangely familiar. But then the moments had passed, and he was left only with memories that he could be certain of. Nor did he trouble himself by trying to make sense of these two moments. He was perfectly content with being a frog.

Now, I must tell you that I know next to nothing about spells or enchantments. We are not living in a time when one *needs* to know anything about them. This is fortunate, in that the need for magical solutions implies the presence of magical dilemmas. The world is more stable than that nowadays. Thoughts create reality only in the subtlest and most comprehensive of ways. We moderns cannot with instantaneous fulfillment wish good to ourselves or harm to our enemies, and the only magic we are likely to encounter is the magic of our young children's sense of the world or the magic of falling in love. For this we can thank our lucky stars.

There are, however, a very few of us who can, for the sake of others, negotiate the journey back and forth between our reality and the borderlands of the soul. I asked a friend of mine who is one of these people (in another culture she would be called a white witch) whether, in her professional opinion, the Frog was under a spell. She told me that my question was irrelevant. "What we know," she said, "is that he was a frog in love with a princess. That's a major predicament. It isn't important how he arrived at it. He might have been a frog with high aspirations, who had an overwhelming desire to leap up the evolutionary ladder. Or he might just as well have been a prince who had forgotten himself. A spell is nothing more than a congealed mind-set. If you *think* you're a frog, you *are* a frog."

And there I will have to leave the matter. We know as little about the Frog's past as the Frog himself did. We know as much about the Princess's past as we need to.

XIV

How She Fell in Love

By now it should be obvious that the fascination of these ancient tales is not so much in what happens as in how and why it happens. We already know what happens. The Condensed Version has been around for a long time, and many of us grew up with it as a benign, monitory presence in the puppet theater of the unconscious. But in a deeper sense, the "how" *is* the "what." Shakespeare's *Hamlet,* to take one famous example, is not the same story (historical-tragical) that old Saxo Grammaticus tells. The Condensed Version, in keeping to the surface of events, leaves the Frog's character an enigma and is especially unfair to the Princess, making her actions seem merely vain and petulant. Her attachment to the golden ball cries out for the explanation I have provided, and later on you will hear in some detail what led to her hurling the Frog against the wall on their wedding night. The important issue at this point is how she came to fall in love.

I will mention only in passing that with this issue a larger and weightier question arises: namely, What makes a woman fall in love with a frog? Many women, since time immemorial, staring up at the bedroom ceiling in the dead middle of the night, have asked themselves the same question, and if I knew the answer I assure you that I would broadcast it freely over the airwaves, without any thought of financial gain, content to be numbered among the supreme benefactors of humankind. I don't know the answer. But I do know how this particular woman fell in love with this particular frog.

Of course, there are frogs and there are frogs. Our frog, as the Princess realized, was a frog with a unique potential. And by no stretch of the imagination could one say that the Princess was lacking in self-esteem.

The fact is that our hero was a very lovable creature. Well, this is not a *fact,* in the strict sense of the word, and there may be those who would deny it, those whose minds, shaped by the scientific culture that is our dominant and often barbarous paradigm, can conceive of the heart merely as a hollow muscular organ which by its rhythmic contraction acts as a force pump for the circulation of the blood (these are the same people who in high-school biology lab took pleasure in pithing and dissecting frogs). But you would have to be very cerebral indeed not to feel any kind of moral attraction to our frog. And in fact—an incontestable fact—the Princess began to love him from the moment she felt the depth of compassion in his first words.

But there was something else besides his compassion and generosity that drew her to him. She was fascinated by his amphibiousness. She herself lived in two elements, the court and the forest. This was nothing, though, compared with a creature who could breathe in either air or water. It was like being able to dwell both in the primal womb of all life and out of it, to move in awareness through both dream and waking consciousness. It seemed to her, upon reflection, that only such a lissome and, as it were, ambidextrous creature could be capable of descending deeply enough to retrieve what was so precious to her.

She was, however, totally unaware that she was falling in love. Her falling was not like the Frog's, who had fallen as if he were standing at the edge of the Grand Canyon and all at once, rapturously, terrifyingly, found himself treading air, then plummeting into the abyss. It was more as if she had stepped on a pebble and lost her balance to such a minuscule degree that she didn't even notice it.

Many elements in the Princess's upbringing

would have rebelled against falling in love with a frog, had she been aware of it. It was ludicrous. It was unworthy of her. Besides being ugly, the Frog was unaccomplished. He couldn't dance or speak Latin or ride a horse or play an instrument. But love, once planted in the heart, is like a mustard seed: though it is the smallest of seeds, it grows and becomes a huge tree and puts forth mighty branches, so that the birds of the sky are able to make their nests in its shade.

Besides, at the beginning of their acquaintance at least, being on good terms with the Frog was, for the Princess, a matter of self-interest. Now, self-interest is usually considered the antithesis of love. But it can just as well be said, and *has* been said by one of the greatest of philosophers, that self-interest is necessarily the ground of our motivation and that love is nourished by nothing so much as by a reasonable self-interest. Charity, after all, begins at home. The Princess, in realizing that the Frog was the only one who could retrieve her golden ball, involuntarily turned her heart in the Frog's direction and placed it in love's way.

"But just a minute," you may be thinking. "Couldn't the Princess have ordered a servant to get her golden ball? Or couldn't she have jumped in and gotten it herself?" The answers are simple. No and no. The Frog was the only one who could retrieve the golden ball because he was the only one who could descend into the well. He was the only one who could descend into the well because the art of diving was still unknown in Europe at this time. The art of diving was still unknown because it had not yet been imported from India. Therefore the Frog was the only one who could retrieve the golden ball. Q.E.D.

XV

The Deal

They had been gazing at each other in silence. The Princess's arms were folded stiffly across her chest. Her look was a resolute stare—glare, one might even say. The Frog looked nervous. He had made a desperate decision.

"Well," the Princess said, "if you are going to be stubborn about it, we might as well change the subject. When were you planning to bring back my golden ball?"

"I could do it any time you wish."

"Now is a good time."

"I can't tell you how long it will take me, you know. I have never done anything like this before. It is a pretty big ball."

The Princess raised her left eyebrow.

"For *me* it is," the Frog said.

"Yes, I suppose so. But let us not quibble about details. You have undertaken this. Therefore you will find a way to do it."

"Mmm, there is one detail that we do have to discuss," the Frog said, looking down.

"And what, pray tell, would that be?"

"There is something . . . There is something I want," the Frog said, forcing himself to meet the Princess's gaze.

"Yes?"

"It is just that . . . Oh, I don't know how to say this gracefully."

"Say it ungracefully then."

The Frog gave a little cough to steady himself. "If I bring you your golden ball, I want something in return."

"Ah. *If* you bring me . . . So it is not a promise. You want to make a deal."

"Well, yes. I suppose that is what you would call it. A deal."

"A business arrangement. Tit for tat."

"If you must put it that way."

"*I* am not putting it that way," said the Princess. "That is the way it is. You say you love me, you will do anything for me, you will get me my golden ball. Oh, and parenthetically, *before* you can get my golden ball, I have to sign a contract with you. Well then, go ahead. What is it?"

"You must agree . . . I am embarrassed to say this . . ." He coughed again. "You must agree to love me and take me as your best friend and let me eat from your plate and drink from your cup and sleep in your bed. I think that is all." He tilted his head and pondered for a moment. "Yes, that is about it."

"And you won't bring me my ball unless I agree to this."

"I really hope that you *will* agree."

"Do I have to make up my mind right now? Or will Your Lordship give me leave to consider your proposal for a little while?"

"Oh, of course, take your time. We have all day."

"Thanks, that is awfully kind of you," said the Princess, with flared nostrils.

As the Princess sat thinking, the Frog sat feeling an intensely uncomfortable mixture of emotions. His heart was still beating fast, and he was having trouble slowing his breath down to its normal, meditative rhythm. He felt relieved that the hardest part of the conversation was over with, and that he had delivered his ultimatum. If she didn't agree to his condition, he had no idea what he would do. He hadn't thought things through to that point and didn't even want to consider the possibility of not helping her. He was proud of himself for having the courage to tell the Princess what he wanted: it wasn't the easiest thing in the world to hold his own before a woman of such indomitable spirits. But he also felt a great wave of sadness washing over him. It pained him that he had to bargain with her, that he was being driven to use even the gentlest kind of force in order to get what he wanted. He hadn't intended to do that. When he had volunteered to retrieve her golden ball, it was solely because he had been so touched by her grief. But things had changed radically since then. He had been laughed at, although he thought he had overcome that obstacle. He had, in addition, been looked at not as the frog he had always supposed himself to be, but as a prince manqué, a person who somehow was willfully refusing to claim his true identity. Because he understood the Princess's character, he was sure that unless he did something drastic this first meeting would be their last. He was ashamed of himself for using power tactics. He was well aware that there would be unfortunate repercussions, and that these would have to be addressed later on, if he and the Princess were in fact meant for each other. A young woman of her mettle couldn't help resenting force of any kind and would certainly look with contempt upon someone who offers help and then, handy-dandy, attaches conditions to the offer like some cheap politician. On the other hand, perhaps someday she would understand the power of his desire and would come to forgive him. Yes, he felt deeply ashamed, but he also felt that he had no choice. He was doing the right thing. He was doing the only possible thing.

Beside him, barely a foot away, the Princess sat trying to contain herself. She was furious. How dare this creature bully her! How dare he demand her love, as if love were a commodity that one could manufacture at will! This little, slimy, goggle-eyed, neckless lump of a thing! What gall he had! Did he think she was some common slut who could be tempted and bought by even the most lucrative of offers? Long flames of rage shot up from her belly to her head.

But what options did she have? She could walk

away and preserve her dignity at the expense of the golden ball. No, that wouldn't work. She *had* to have her golden ball back. That much was clear.

Or perhaps she could try to persuade the Frog to take back his condition and renew his original offer, which had been so very simple and generous. She wished that she had formally accepted it when it had first been made. But she hadn't taken it seriously, had barely heard it, in her bereft and distracted state of mind. And now the moment was past. Furthermore, how could she persuade anyone of anything in her present state? And even if she were feeling absolutely calm, there was nothing to be said. All rational arguments would be useless. She had seen the determination in the little creature's eyes. Of course, there was a chance that she could move him to a further level of compassion by pleading with him, or by play-acting, bursting into tears again so that he might relent. But these were tactics just as contemptible as the Frog's revised offer.

Nor would she consider using her physical attractiveness to get what she wanted. She had never acted seductively, at least to her knowledge. Certainly she had not fluttered her eyelashes at any man or tried to charm any woman. Even when she had been at odds with her father or mother, she had always won them over to her point of view (when she did win them over) by the power and clarity of her thinking.

There *were* no options. She would have to agree to the Frog's condition. Exactly how she could manage to keep her word was, for the time being, unclear to her. She wouldn't have a problem letting the Frog eat from her plate and drink from her cup. She was not squeamish like most of the ladies at court. And even the clause about letting him sleep in her bed would not present an insurmountable difficulty, she thought. Her bed was a large one, king-size in fact: there would be plenty of room for him on one side of the mattress or at its foot. Since she was not a restless sleeper, there would be little danger that she might roll over and crush him.

But to love him, to take him as her best friend: how could she manage that? If he was an enchanted prince, of course, there might be no problem—*if,* that is, she could figure out a way to disenchant him, and if, once liberated from his froggish form, he turned out to be a prince she *could* love. But suppose she was wrong about him. No, she wasn't wrong: with such a powerful intuition she couldn't be wrong. But just suppose. Suppose he was no more than a compassionate talking frog. What kind of best friend and bed-companion could he be? There must be a way. It would take serious consideration. She was still angry. But once she made her decision, she knew, the impossible would become possible and the solution would somehow appear. That was how things had happened in the past. That was how the universe worked, with an intelligence so vast that it took her breath away. She didn't have to figure things out. She could accept the Frog's offer in good conscience, and leave the rest to the . . .

XVI

The Deal Concluded

"... Tao," said the Princess.

"What happened?" the Frog said.

"Nothing. I was just thinking."

"Oh. Good. I was afraid something stung you. A bee or a wasp."

"If anything stung me, it was you."

"I am sorry."

"Sorry enough to let go of your demand?"

"I am truly sorry, but I have to insist on that. It is the only way."

"I thought so. You are a very stubborn fellow."

"Almost as stubborn as you, dear Princess. If I may say so without disrespect."

"I have heard the term used in reference to me. In my case it simply means 'determined.'"

"Precisely. We are very much alike."

"Hmpf!" the Princess said.

"Anyway, have you made up your mind?"

"Yes, I have. I am not overjoyed about it, but I will agree to your condition."

"Wonderful. I am very glad to hear that. Let us shake hands on it." He raised himself a little, leaned backward, and held out his right arm. The Princess took the small, four-fingered hand between her thumb and her index finger and shook it, gently. It was impossible to keep from smiling.

"What is so amusing?" the Frog said.

"We *are* very much alike," said the Princess.

The Frog nodded. "Well, I had better be going. I will be back as soon as I can."

"Good luck."

"Your faithful servant," he said, lowering the

front of his body in an ungainly bow. With a jump he was another foot away from her. With a second jump he was gone.

The Princess saw him disappear, then watched the ripples as they spread out to the edge of the well.

XVII

Bringing Back the Golden Ball

$\mathcal{L}$ower and lower the Frog descends. His nostrils are closed. He kicks with his webbed feet. He is headed straight down.

Swimming to the bottom of the well is like moving through a dream: in the denser atmosphere, everything feels charged with meaning. His breath becomes lighter, fuller, moves out over the whole surface of his body. His skin tingles with aliveness. His blood starts to leap. Down, down, deeper, darker, until he can smell the mud.

The Frog touches bottom. He looks around. In

the dim light he sees nothing but water and mud. Where could the Princess's ball be?

He takes a few steps to the right, vertically suspended like a ballet dancer. He looks again. Ah. There, a little farther on: a glimmer. He swims over to it. Yes, it is the golden ball, half buried in the mud. He can see its seam and the small golden clasp. What should he do now?

He gives it a push with his nose. Nothing. It doesn't budge. He digs his feet into the mud, steadies himself, then pushes harder, with nose and arms. The ball rolls.

Now what?

The ball is four inches across: almost as large as his whole body. Can he pick it up in his mouth? Hmm. Unlikely, but worth a try. He opens his mouth wide and attempts to get a grip on the smooth golden surface. Wider, wider. But his jaws begin to ache. This is useless.

He sits back and considers the situation. The only possible method, it seems, is to get beneath the ball and lift it up as he himself rises. His balance will have to be perfect. He will have to concentrate hard. But it is doable.

He pushes his nose under the ball. It rolls onto his forehead, then rolls off to the left, back into the mud. He tries this ten more times. Ten times the ball rolls off.

The eleventh time he succeeds in balancing it on a point slightly in front of his eyes. He swims up through the water slowly, slowly.

As he nears the surface, just as he is picturing how happy the Princess will be, the ball rolls off. He sees it sink, then dives down after it.

XVIII

The Kiss

(1)

"No, I wasn't about to give up on you," the Princess said. "But I didn't expect you to take so long. You must have been down there for at least two hours." She was sitting on the well's rim, with her legs tucked under her. On her lap, in a fold of her velvet skirt, lay the golden ball. A few drops of water glistened from its surface.

"It was a difficult task," the Frog said. "I am very glad that you are pleased with me."

"I am, I am. I can't tell you how excited I was,

after all that waiting, when I saw my golden ball surface from the well, all by itself it seemed. And then you, balancing it on the end of your nose like a trained seal."

"But without any training. It was very hard to keep it balanced. I was afraid that it would fall off again, at the last moment, before I could give it to you."

"Well, it was awfully clever of you to surface right where I was sitting," the Princess said. "I just had to lean over and pluck the ball from your hands . . . from your nose, I mean."

"Yes. It is still a bit muddy, the ball. I hope it hasn't soiled your skirt."

"Oh, I don't mind a little mud. What is important is that I have my golden ball back. How can I ever thank you?"

"You know how."

"Oh, that. Yes, we will get to that in good time. But I am so happy right now. I feel like celebrating."

"How shall we celebrate?"

"Let us drink a toast. There is no champagne, so we will use water."

"All right."

The Princess scooped up a handful of water with her right hand, then poured a little onto her left palm. "Here," she said, holding it out to the Frog. "You may drink from this."

"And may I propose a toast?" the Frog said. "To your happiness."

"Thank you," the Princess said. "To my happiness and independence." She raised her cupped right hand to her mouth and drank. The Frog sipped from her left palm.

"And now," said the Princess, "I am going home. But not before I do this." She leaned over, steadying herself on her elbow, and lowered her head until she was face to face with the Frog. Then she kissed him on his cold lips.

Five seconds passed.

Ten seconds.

Nothing happened.

After a minute, she sat up and glared. "I am very disappointed in you, I must say."

"But why, Princess? I haven't done a thing."

"That is exactly the point. You had your chance, and you didn't do a thing."

"What was I *supposed* to do?"

"Oh, you know very well," the Princess said, in a tone of great disgust. "You think that you are really a frog. I don't believe it for a single moment. But I can't solve your problem *for* you. And I am certainly not going to try kissing you again. Ugh!"

"What problem?"

But the Princess—with no intention of breaking her promise, but feeling no obligation to keep it just yet—had already stood up and begun walking back to the palace in long, impatient strides.

"Wait, Princess!" the Frog shouted. "Wait for me!"

The Princess didn't hear him. The only sound she heard was the quick, determined crunch of pebbles beneath her feet.

XIX

Pride and Precedents

At the beginning of our story, I described the Princess as "proud, ungrateful, and headstrong." We have now arrived at a point where this statement must be qualified. It is not untrue. But it needs to be placed in the proper context for its truth to be seen disinterestedly and not as a moral judgment.

We all know stories in which a young woman of wit, high spirits, and a discriminating heart doesn't hesitate to say no to a proposal that comes from a man who is, in sexual terms, the archetypal frog—whom only the dull, the fearful, or the altruistic would accept as a husband. A young woman like this knows her own value. She would not think of compromising it, even at the risk of dispossessing her entire family.

What may appear to be proud, ungrateful, and headstrong from the outside may from the inside express an unshakable integrity of character. Pride, if it doesn't step over the line into arrogance, is simply an unprejudiced self-esteem. Ingratitude is the appropriate response to a kindness that has hooks on it. *Headstrong* is another word for trusting your own heart.

It is important to be clear about this point, because we are coming now to a crucial matter. What does the Princess want?

She wants to be met. She wants to engage, in all parts of her body and soul, with a partner who is her equal. That is, she wants what any reasonably self-interested woman wants.

From the Frog's perspective, the Princess's desire seems reasonable as long as it doesn't refer to him. If she expects *him* to be her equal, she is completely out of her gourd. What he wants is to be loved for who he is, not for who he may conceivably become. He values himself, but he also knows his limits. If he is expected to meet the Princess on all levels of herself, he feels doomed to failure. He is aware that certain of his talents—the ability to dive deep, for example—may be of essential help to the well-being of her soul. But what kind of life can he live with her at court, or even in her wished-for cottage in the forest, while she is occupied with so many modes of beauty that he can never hope to be part of? There is also the question of embracing her. The very thought of it makes him feel so incapable that he is ready to drown in his own despair, if frogs could drown.

From the perspective of an outsider, the Princess's expectation seems not merely insane but unkind as well. The first rule of love is to accept the other person fully, just as he is. Right?

Wrong. The Princess is a woman of vision. She *sees* that the Frog is a prince. She doesn't care how he got to be a frog, and she won't waste her time figuring out how he can become a prince. But she is certain that one way or another he can transform himself. She refuses to accept him as who he temporarily is, because she knows who he truly is. For her to accept him as a frog would be to deny her vision. That she will not do.

In any other situation, the Princess's expectation would constitute cruelty to talking animals. But we know how our story ends. The Frog actually does turn into a prince, and it is because of the Princess's visionary stubbornness. More about this later. What you should realize now is that if our heroine had been a kinder, gentler princess, she would have wound up with nothing but a pet frog.

XX

The Journey of a Thousand Miles Begins with the First Hop

The Frog sits on the rim of the well. The Princess has long since gone. He keeps staring into the forest, toward the point where she disappeared among the maple trees.

He knows that sooner or later he will follow her back to the palace.

It is a very long way.

He had better begin.

But a strange inertia has overtaken him. He feels incapable of movement. He feels incapable of anything.

Occasionally a thought buzzes through his mind like a fat fly. He watches it come and go, without moving.

The King,
the Queen

While the Frog was gathering his courage to begin the long journey to the palace, the Princess's mother and father, having concluded their affairs of state for the day, had repaired to the royal study. The Queen was arranging roses in a dozen large celadon vases that had been imported from Korea in her great-grandfather's time. The study was the King's sanctuary, and she made sure that everything in it was always comme il faut. Its walnut panels had, during the previous century, been carved by Italian craftsmen with scenes from the history of Greece,

Rome, and China: Pericles delivering the Funeral Oration, Lao-tzu dictating to the border guard, the boy Alexander taming Bucephalus by easing him away from his own shadow, Horace pruning grapevines on his beloved Sabine farm, Li Po and Tu Fu on a lakeside terrace raising their wine cups to the moon. Books bound in gold-tooled purple morocco lined the shelves. Some were illuminated manuscripts, others were printed on vellum; and in the corners of their exquisitely decorated frontispieces, as well as inside the lavish capital letters that began each chapter, the finest miniaturists of their day had painted portraits of the King's or the Queen's ancestors in easy companionship with the ancient authors: Aristotle playing chess with the Queen's great-grandfather, for example, or Chuang-tzu and Confucius dining at the high table of the King's father. Between the bookcases, afternoon sunlight fell through high, stained-glass windows onto armchairs upholstered in purple velvet and onto the King's desk, which was inlaid with alternating gold-leaf and mother-of-pearl fleurs-de-lys and supported by four recumbent ebony lions whose benign smiles implied that they had just finished a good meal.

The King was sitting on one of the armchairs, reading Pliny's *Naturalis Historia* in a hand-finished copy of the superb Nicolas Jenson edition. The Queen was arranging the last of the roses.

"Is it just me," she said, turning to the King, "or do you feel that something unusual is about to happen?"

"No," said the King, "everything seems quite ordinary, thank heaven."

"It is a very uncomfortable sensation. I wish you felt it, too."

"Well, my love, perhaps this will turn out to be one of your *in*accurate premonitions. Do your earlobes itch?"

"Just the left one."

"Hmm. Not a clear sign. We will have to wait and see. Of course, even if it *were* a clear sign, we would have to wait and see."

"Yes, but we would be waiting differently."

"In alert mode," the King said. "It is quite a while since the last Unusual Phenomenon happened in our kingdom."

"Almost five years."

"And how passionately we all hope that that was the final one."

"But then, of course, there is the report from Germany. They have had two incidents during the past three years."

"Yes, that report *was* distressing. Especially the item about the two children in the Black Forest."

"And the house made of gingerbread."

"And that cannibal woman with the tiny red eyes," the King said. "Brrr. It still makes my flesh creep."

"The other item was almost as grim."

"The one about the golden bird?"

"Oh, there was more than a golden bird," the Queen said. "There was a golden horse and a girl in a golden castle. A girl with a good pedigree, I am happy to say. The prince managed to bring them all home. Actually, that prince is the third and youngest son of the King of Wittenberg, your second cousin once removed."

"My cousin always did consider his youngest son something of a dimwit. Before the incident, that is. It was a *very* unusual affair."

"Yes, dear, it was. Things got quite gruesome toward the end, but it all turned out well, as most of these incidents do."

"But even when they end well, the whole kingdom walks around with frayed nerves for months afterward. People can't pass an animal without feeling spied upon. They begin to talk in whispers whenever a horse or a cow approaches. They stop eating meat. The price of vegetables soars."

"Not to mention the price of rings."

"Is your earlobe still itching?"

"Both of them are."

"Still," said the King, "that is not a definitive sign. You are mistaken nine times out of ten, after all."

"It is more like five out of six, I think. But you are right. I admit that I am often mistaken. I just hope this has nothing to do with [here she mentioned the Princess's given name]."

"Where is she this afternoon?"

"Oh, she is probably walking somewhere in the forest."

"She is at a peculiar age. I am sure that she will grow out of it."

"I certainly hope so," the Queen said. "She is twenty-three. It is high time for her to marry and settle down. We should never have consented to her Test."

"Don't worry," said the King. "It will all work out. She will fall in love when she is ready. The right man will come along."

XXII

Yellow Alert

It was a very long time before the Frog managed to arrive at the gates of the palace. The Condensed Version says that the journey took him a day. But what appears as a single day to a human being may be a month or a year in the consciousness of a small animal. Besides, old stories are famously cavalier in their measurement of time. By *day* they may mean not the period between one sunrise and the next, but something magnified beyond our ability to grasp it, something that bears the same relation to our experience of "one day" as a mountain does to a pebble chipped off from it. Thus, when the Book of Genesis tells us that there was evening and there was morning, a first day—although the sun did not yet exist and would not exist until the fourth "day"—we see the very bedrock of language in a state of molten fluidity, and ourselves standing in the Garden, shoulder to shoulder with Adam, before anything on this earth had discovered its proper name.

Eventually, however, the Frog did arrive. Stair by huge stair he hopped up the granite staircase leading from the woods to the formal garden. Stair by huge stair he hopped up the granite staircase leading from the formal garden to the front gates of the palace. Finally, after passing through the gates, through the front entrance, and through the reception hall, he collapsed in a green heap, panting, not far from the great oaken door of the dining room.

On the other side of the door, in the magnificent cobalt-violet dining hall that had been the Queen's greatest vexation and glory, the royal family were seated at the smallest of the four tables. A string trio, stationed near the passageway to the kitchen, played a suite of dinner music with an ardor balanced by their discretion. The King sat at the table's head, the Queen to his right, and the Princess to his left, across from him at a distance of about seven feet: not an intimate distance, but close enough so that she didn't have to raise her voice. A tablecloth of rich, ivory-white damask covered the inlaid mahogany. All the dinnerware was fashioned of twenty-four-karat gold (it had to be melted down and recast whenever there was a serious dent): the massive plates, the water cups and the wine cups, the heavy knives, spoons, and three-tined forks, all of them molded with the royal symbols of key and serpent. The gold glowed in the light of the candelabras and seemed to the King and Queen as commonplace and to-be-taken-for-granted as fired clay and stainless steel would seem to us, so elastic are the outlines of human desire.

The menu as well was an everyday affair. After the half dozen hors d'œuvres, which included frogs' legs today, three liveried waiters had brought out three golden platters of crêpes filled with sliced lobster and chanterelles to begin the dinner itself, along with a bottle of fine Chardonnay. The next course, which had been served just five minutes before, was turbot roasted with champagne and leeks. For the remainder of the meal—after a taste-cleansing interlude of lemon sherbet—the chef had prepared poached squab stuffed with turnips, sage, and foie gras of duck, and a leg of lamb with caramelized endives and truffle sauce, accompanied by an old Burgundy. Finally, with the cheese cart and fruit, there would be a bottle of champagne and one of vintage port, and, for dessert, a double-chocolate cake with chocolate mousse and/or an apple-and-almond tart with vanilla-bean gelato. The King and Queen were not great believers in austerity.

The dinner conversation proceeded in its usual

witty and learned way, from philosophy to politics to architecture to the bloodlines of the royal stallions to a famous collection of antique cameos that the King was negotiating to buy from the Duke of Milan. But beneath the level of the words, the Queen's mind was, let us say, on yellow alert. She had observed that the Princess had been acting in an unusually buoyant manner today, and this, along with her own itching earlobes, gave her pause. Something had happened to the Princess; she was sure of it. And something was about to happen. What in the world could it be?

The Princess's face was usually animated, but the animation that the Queen noticed in it now was at a higher intensity—as if, amid the talk of philosophy, cameos, and horses, the Princess were bursting with an intellectual discovery she had just made. The irises of her eyes, a rich burnt umber that lightened infinitesimally as it approached the pupils, were almost giving off sparks. The Queen had seen her in this state of mind half a dozen times before, had watched with a mixture of pleasure, concern, and incomprehension, though in none of these instances had she been able, by indirections, to learn what the excitement was all about. It had taken a great deal of tact and self-control not to ask, even when the Princess was a child. The Queen was not about to ask now.

XXIII

Serenade

Before there were humans, before there were mammals, before there were feathered birds, when nature had been listening to her own silence for billions of years and the only sounds were wind sounds and water sounds and the dull buzz of insects, out of the mouths of frogs arose the first song on earth. And though there have been more melodious songs since then (the songs of nightingale and mocking-bird, of porpoise and whale, of Bach and Mozart and Schubert), there is no song—now, in the days of earth's peril, when so many of their species have vanished, serving as the planet's white corpuscles who lay down their lives in the struggle against human greed and folly—there is no song more worthy of our respect than the ancient song of the frog.

Frogs themselves, of course, believe that their song is second to none. What sounds to us like *ribbit* or *brekekekek ko-ax ko-ax* is to them, and perhaps to a discerning suprahuman ear, the most beautiful and erotic of serenades. That is why Aristophanes' chorus of frogs, modestly yet emphatically, tells us how favored they are by all the gods of music and poetry:

> For the Muses have graced us with their own
>   sweet, heart-soothing voices;
> and Pan, the horned walker, who whistles
>   through a reed in the woods,
> delights in our song, and Apollo himself
>   is enthralled
> when we choir in rivers and ponds, as we
>   wriggle among

the marshflowers or bask on green lilypads in
the sunlight;
and even when it rains and we dive down into
deep water,
you can still hear our music bubbling up from
below.

The Frog is sitting outside the great oaken door of the dining room. He knows that the Princess is inside. He is determined to hold her to their agreement, though he doesn't want to be heavy-handed or legalistic about it. He realizes that she is still physically revolted by him. On the other hand, she has only heard him speak. He has never yet sung to her.

He takes a large gulp of air. He closes his mouth and nostrils. He squeezes the air back and forth between his lungs and mouth, forcing some of it through the slits in the floor of his mouth and into his vocal sac, which inflates like a balloon. Then he lets loose. He is in particularly fine voice today. The most ravishing cadences and trills issue from his throat. He sings all the emotions that have made his heart full to overflowing: his love for the Princess, his longing and discouragement, his confusion, his absurd hope. He feels energized— inspired. He sings on and on, can barely stop for another gulp of air. Song after glorious song resonates through the dining room, through the reception hall, through the living quarters, through the whole vast echoing palace, and out into the echoing air.

XXIV

The King, the Queen, the Princess, the Frog

"What is that awful croaking?" said the Queen.

"If it weren't so improbable," the King said, "I would think there was some sort of frog or toad at the door." Then, turning to the Princess: "Do you know anything about this?"

The Princess blushed. "Yes, Papà. There *is* a frog at the door. I will explain everything later."

"Well then, my dear," the King said, "please get up and do something about the noise."

"Yes, Papà," the Princess said. She folded her embroidered damask napkin and laid it beside her plate. Then, as a waiter pulled back her chair, she stood up, walked to the door, and opened it.

The Frog deflated his vocal sac. He bowed to her, then hopped over the threshold. "Good afternoon," he said in a loud voice. "I hope that Your Highness is very well."

"Thank you," the Princess said. "I certainly didn't expect to see you here. It must have been a long trip."

"A very long trip indeed," the Frog said. Then, to the King: *"Sire, je suis très-heureux de faire votre connoissance royale."* And with a deep bow to the Queen: "Majesty. Your humble servant."

The King was embarrassed. It was obvious that an Unusual Phenomenon had begun to take place: not only in his kingdom, not only in his capital, not only in his palace, but right in the middle of his own family. He could feel his stomach swirling as if the room were a ship in a storm. On the other hand, the Frog was obviously a well-brought-up creature. His French was superb. There was no reason not to treat him like any other intelligent being, to extend to him the same courtesy one would extend to a nobleman or even to an educated bourgeois. In spite of the fact that this event was most unwelcome—was in fact the last thing in the world that he would have wished to happen—the King was aware that only someone who is ready for everything, who doesn't exclude any experience, even the most incomprehensible, can really be said to be living in harmony with the Tao. Yes, the Master "is available to all people / and doesn't reject anyone, / is ready to use all situations / and doesn't waste anything." The King hoped that he could undergo this event with even a small part of that masterly grace.

"Good afternoon, sir," he said to the Frog with a nod of acknowledgment. "Welcome to our palace."

The Queen said nothing. There was nothing on her face.

The King turned to her. "My love, our visitor has wished us a good afternoon."

"Ah," said the Queen, blinking as if she had just come out of a trance. "Good day, sir. A good day to you. How are you today?"

"Actually," the Frog said, "I am feeling very tired and very hungry."

"In that case, you must join us at our meal," the King said. "You may sit beside my daughter, since you two seem to be acquainted."

"Thank you, Your Majesty. That is most kind of you. I would be grateful for some food."

"Pick him up, my dear," the King said to the Princess. "Bring him to your place and put him on the table beside you."

The Princess obeyed, with a shudder that only

the Frog could notice. As she walked back to the table, the King rang the small golden dinner bell that stood to the right of his plate.

The door to the kitchen opened and out came the chef, a short, angular man in white, wearing a white silk apron. He bowed, walked to the head of the table, and bowed again.

"We have a dinner guest today," the King said.

The chef turned in the direction of the Princess, glanced at the visitor, and with perfect sang-froid said, "Yes, Your Majesty."

"I don't know our guest's preferences," the King said, "but I suppose that *mouches à l'orange* would not be unwelcome. Have the sous-chef go out and hunt for a dozen large flies."

"At your service, Your Majesty," the chef said, with a bow. "I will prepare a dish fit, as it were, for a king."

Twenty minutes later, after an interlude of small talk that went into great detail about the weather that spring, the dish was brought out and set before the Frog. On a small golden plate,

inside an archipelago of watercress and diced garlic, twelve flies, broiled medium rare, their crisp
little legs sticking straight up, floated on their
backs in a fragrant, orange-brown sea.

At the very moment when this dish was set
onto the table, the waiters, with precision chore-
ography, snatched away the plates of turbot, now
grown cold, and replaced them with plates of
poached squab.

The King and Queen picked up their knives
and forks and began to eat. After the second fork-
ful, the King turned to the Frog and said, "Why
haven't you begun, sir? Is the dish not to your
liking?"

"On the contrary, Your Majesty, it both looks
and smells delicious. But Her Highness and I have
entered into a small agreement. I would not pre-
sume to broach the subject myself."

"My dear, what is the gentleman—mmm, the
gentlefrog—referring to?" the King said.

"Oh, Papà," the Princess said, blushing again.
(Her blush was extremely attractive, the Frog

thought.) "It is true. This frog and I did make a . . . an arrangement."

"What kind of arrangement?"

"Well, Papà, somehow I dropped my golden ball into the well, and this frog offered to bring it back for me. In return," she said, lowering her eyes and voice, "I agreed . . . Well, I agreed to love him and take him as my best friend and let him eat from my plate and drink from my cup and . . ."—her voice was very faint now—"and sleep in my bed."

"You did what?!" the Queen said.

"Her Highness agreed," said the Frog, "to love me, and to take me as her best friend, and to let me eat from her golden plate, drink from her golden cup, and sleep in her own soft bed. That is why I am waiting for her to transfer my—I must say, elegantly prepared—*mouches* onto her plate, or at least to put them on its rim."

"You did what?!!" the Queen said, at an even higher pitch of agitation.

"Please don't be upset, Mamà," the Princess said. "You know how I treasure my golden ball. The frog was willing to get it, if I agreed to his terms. It seemed the only possible solution."

"The issue," said the King, "is not whether this was the only possible solution. The fact is . . . The fact is . . . Oh, do get a grip on yourself, my love." A sound somewhere between a scream and a sob was trying to find its way out of the Queen's throat.

"The fact is," the Frog said, "that Her Highness made me a promise."

"Precisely," the King said. "You have hit the nail on its proverbial head. Whether or not the promise should have been made is irrelevant. Whether Her Highness's judgment in making it was sound or unsound is equally irrelevant. The fact is that she gave her word. Our word is the lifeblood of our honor, the very soul of our integrity. And if we, who are at what is both the foundation and the apex of society, should fail to keep our word, only disaster can follow, a disaster far worse than the petty disasters that arrive in the course of nature and from which one can always either physically or morally recuperate. If we, who live and die by our sacred honor, should fail to honor our word, solemnly or even casually given, the bonds that hold society together would unravel: the nobility would lose heart, the bourgeoisie would no longer be guided by our example, the poor would stop dreaming of us, neighbor would begin to cheat neighbor, husband would lie to wife, and the whole of human fellowship would turn into nothing more than a pack of snarling animals. I beg your pardon."

"No offense taken," the Frog said. "Your Majesty's eloquence would charm even the most savage of beasts."

"Thank you, sir," the King said. "A very handsome compliment."

"If I may interrupt, Papà," the Princess said.

"Yes, my dear," the King said. "You may speak."

"I never intended to break my promise," the Princess said.

"Then why," said the Frog, "did you run away from me? You left me at the well, and it took me an awfully long time to catch up."

"I am sorry about that. I truly am. But I was so happy yesterday that I just wanted to celebrate."

"And what about your promise?" the King said.

"I was intending to keep it, I assure you. But I needed some time to myself first, to let it sink in. After all, our agreement didn't state that everything had to happen all at once."

"Is that true?" the King said to the Frog.

"Yes, Your Majesty, certainly that was not stated. But, with your gracious permission, I would very much like to present my side of the story."

"By all means, sir. Continue," the King said.

"If *I* may interrupt," the Queen said.

"Our guest made his request first, my love," the

King said, "and it is only courteous to let him speak. After he is finished, you may say whatever you like."

The Queen nodded. She was looking very unhappy.

"Here is my case, Your Majesty," the Frog said. "I have been in love with your daughter for some time now. I realize, of course, that I am altogether unworthy of her and that she lives on an infinitely higher plane than I do. On the other hand, I am an enormously . . . let us say, determined fellow. I have many virtues that may not be immediately apparent when you look at my outward form. And I think that I have much to offer Her Highness."

"Would you care to be specific?" said the King.

"Not really, Your Majesty, if that is permissible. Her Highness is well aware of what I have to offer. The Test of the Three Balls—I heard about it from a certain fox—would be a mere formality with me. I know which one to choose."

"It sounds as if you have made a proposal of marriage," the King said.

"It was and is a proposal," the Frog said. "That is obvious."

Another scream/sob tried to force its way out of the Queen's throat.

"Close your eyes, my love," the King said. "Breathe. You will have your chance, as soon as our guest is finished."

"Let me tell you exactly how things happened at the well," the Frog said. "Her Highness was distraught, poor dear, and was crying her eyes out. It would have taken a hard heart indeed not to fall at her feet and offer her anything in the world that might ease her pain. I wasn't certain that I could bring back her golden ball, but I was willing to die in the attempt. And I would have done far more had she asked me to. I would have hopped to the ends of the earth, hunted for golden keys, outwitted evil magicians, sorted through mountains of grain, called on the whole animal kingdom to help me accomplish whatever task had been set for me. That is how deeply I love her, and how sure I am that we are meant to be together."

"Then why did you place a condition on your love?" the King said.

"Yes, why did you force me into an agreement?" the Princess said. Her voice was a glowing filament.

"It seemed like the only way to ensure what *had* to happen," the Frog said. "I will pay for it later, I know. But I also know that your anger will soften as your love for me grows. Love softens everything except our sense of integrity."

"Hmm," said the King. "I must write that down in my book of aphorisms. I don't know if it is deep, but it *sounds* deep. So you did manage to bring back the golden ball."

"Yes. It was a difficult task, but not an impossible one. I was proud of myself. And I was very happy for Her Highness. But after a brief celebration, and a briefer, not wholly satisfactory kiss, she turned on her heels and ran away. I realize that she needed some time by herself to take in everything that had happened. But, if I may make a slight criticism of someone whom I otherwise hold in the highest esteem, it seems a trifle discourteous of her not to have consulted me first. She could easily have said, 'Look, Frog'—she calls me Frog—'I need some time alone to sort all this out. Let us meet here again tomorrow. I will invite you to the palace as soon as I possibly can, and introduce you to my parents, and then we will start eating, drinking, and sleeping together.' That would have been the proper way to proceed. Don't you think so, Your Majesty?"

"Yes, I do," said the King. "I certainly do."

"Well, that is how things look from my perspective," the Frog said. "I hope that Your Majesty will see fit to grant me your daughter's hand in marriage." Then, turning to the Queen: "I hope this is agreeable to you as well, Your Majesty."

"I am trying . . . ," the Queen said, "I am trying very hard . . . to maintain my sense of composure." Anxiety had taken hold of her nervestrings like a puppeteer.

"Splendid, my love," the King said. "That is all we can ask of you."

"But it is not easy to sit here and witness these events—*unusual* is hardly a strong enough word for them—spin so quickly out of control." She paused for a few moments, then turned to the Frog. "Now, sir, let me say, first of all, that you seem to be an excellent person . . . creature. I have nothing against you *per se.*"

"*Per te,*" said the King.

"*Per te.* In fact, I am touched both by your love for my daughter and by your strength of character. I wish nothing more for Her Highness than that she find a good man who truly loves her. And there, precisely, is the rub. You are not a man. You are a frog."

"We know that, my love," the King said.

"Papà . . . ," the Princess said.

"Just one moment," the Queen said. "We know that, yet we are acting as if we didn't know it at all. Have we even begun to think out the consequences of this . . . union? I would have no problem at all, I assure you, if marriage meant simply companionship. You are old enough, [here she called the

Princess by her given name], to make your choice on your own, and if I felt satisfied with your prospective husband's loyalty and goodness of heart, that would be the end of the matter. Of course, I would have wished for someone a bit taller, a bit less . . . green."

"I am dreadfully sorry, Your Majesty," the Frog said.

"Not at all, not at all," the Queen said. "This is not about your outward appearance. Or it has very little to do with it. But the fact is that marriage means more than companionship. It also means children, or the possibility of children."

"And Your Majesty is upset by the prospect?" the Frog said.

"My dear sir," said the Queen. "I am trying to be large-minded about this whole affair. Neither by nature nor by upbringing am I someone who holds to narrow views of the world, or whose prejudices—if I have prejudices—are able to exercise any dominance over her thinking. While I may not always succeed at being reasonable, I at least make every possible effort. Now, it is true that I have imagined my future son-in-law as being tall, handsome, and French. Or if not French, at least Western European. Or if not Western European, at least human. That may have been shortsighted of me, but it is understandable, I think. I can let go of such imaginings, and I can consciously try to broaden my esthetics to include what, in your species, may be considered a particular sign of beauty: the precise angle at which your eyeballs bulge out of your head, perhaps, or the degree of translucency of your clammy white throat."

"Very kind of you, Your Majesty," the Frog said, with a small bow. "Though I doubt that I am a handsome specimen even among frogs."

"That is not the point," said the Queen. "The point is that you are a person . . . a creature . . . of character, and I would be happy to welcome you into my family, to give you my sincere blessing, if it weren't for the question of offspring."

"And what exactly is your objection, my love?" the King said.

"Isn't it obvious?"

"I am afraid not," the King said. "I don't quite see what you are driving at."

"Heavens above!" said the Queen. "Just think of it! My grandchildren—*our* grandchildren— would be half-human and half-frog!"

"True," the King said. "Certainly that is true. But it does not pose an insuperable difficulty, it seems to me. They will, you know, have a mother and a father who have excellent characters and kind hearts. And frogs, like beavers, seals, and other amphibians, as Pliny tells us, are very versatile creatures. In any event, I would much prefer that our daughter marry this frog than that she marry either of those beautiful, shiftless elder sons of the King of Wittenberg, for example."

"Who happen to be dead now," the Queen said.

"Mmm, yes, you are right. But you see my point. The Frog's skin may be green, but his heart is red."

"The fact is, however," said the Queen, "that our grandchildren would be monsters."

"Monsters?" the King said. "I am not so sure. There is nothing either good or bad, after all, but thinking makes it so. They may turn out to be very pretty children. The mermaids, for example, who are half-human and half-fish, are famous for their beauty. I don't see why children with our daughter's top half and our son-in-law's bottom half would be any less attractive."

"But what assurance is there," said the Queen, "that nature would sort them out that way? It is just as likely that they would have our daughter's bottom half and our son-in-law's top half. In either event, they would be freaks of nature, poor things. Like those maladjusted, never-satisfied satyrs. Or like Pasiphaë's raging son, the Minotaur."

"May I say something?" the Princess said.

"Yes, of course, my dear," the King said, "but let your mother and me finish our discussion first." Then, to the Queen: "On the other hand, there is the example of Chiron. I would consider myself blessed if a grandchild of mine turned out to be even half as distinguished as that very distinguished centaur."

"That is true. I hadn't thought of that. How proud his grandparents must have been!"

"I wonder if they ever visited his school at the summit of Mount Pelion, where he taught astronomy, music, botany, and medicine. What extraordinary students were attracted to him there! Heracles. Jason. Odysseus. Theseus. Achilles. And when he died, he became a distinguished constellation, which contains the solar system's closest neighbor in space: Alpha Centauri, the third brightest star in the sky. Only Sirius and Canopus are brighter."

"I see your point," said the Queen. "Perhaps not all mixed marriages have problematic offspring. Perhaps I am exaggerating the problem."

"And we have not yet mentioned the gods of Egypt," said the King, "who furnish even more luminous examples of the excellence of the half-human. There are, among others, Osiris's son

Anubis, half-jackal, half-man, who guides souls to the realm of the dead; Hathor, the cow-headed goddess of love and mirth; Sekhmet, goddess of the sun, both woman and lioness; and the god of day, Horus, with his fierce-eyed hawk's head. What further proof could you require?"

"Yes, yes," the Queen said. "And yet how very strange it all seems. I can't help but be a little disappointed. I would have preferred a Valois or a Montmorency as a son-in-law. Preferably one with shapely legs."

"Really, my love!" the King said. "Given the time, the place, and the menu, that is hardly a tactful remark."

"I beg your pardon, sir," the Queen said.

"Majesty," said the Frog with a small bow.

"In any event," the King said, "even if our grandchild is, as you put it, a monster, he may turn out to be a Chiron or a Horus."

"But a hawk's head on our grandchild has a certain dignity," the Queen said, "a certain elegance, that would make his presentation at court not impossible. A hawk's head is one thing. A frog's head is quite another."

"Oh, my love," the King said, "a frog's head would be no more ridiculous than the skinny, long-beaked head of an ibis that Thoth bears with pride. The master of wisdom and magic. And truly, versed in the Tao Te Ching as you are, you should know better. 'When people see some things as beautiful, / other things become ugly.'"

"'Things arise,'" the Queen said, with a meditative drawl, "'and she lets them come, / things disappear and she lets them go.' You are right. I stand corrected, and I am willing to withdraw my objection. Our grandchild is just as likely to be wise as if he had two human parents."

"Or just as likely to be a fool," the King said.

"Papà, may I speak now?" said the Princess.

"Yes, we are finished. What have you been wanting to say?"

"Well, Papà, it is sweet of you to be so deeply

interested in the welfare of my future children, and I am as touched as I am annoyed by your and Mamà's concern. But since you have not understood the most important point of all, your whole discussion is irrelevant."

"What do you mean?" the King said.

"What important point?" the Queen said.

"This may seem like a mixed marriage . . . ," the Princess said.

"It certainly does," the King said, looking from the Princess to the Frog and back to the Princess. The Queen nodded.

"But the point is that this frog is in reality a human being. A prince, in fact," the Princess said.

"Is that true, sir?" the King said.

The Frog shrugged his not very prominent shoulders. "Her Highness is convinced of it," he said. "I have a hard time believing it myself."

"Of *course* it is true," the Princess said. "And everyone can stop worrying about children. Our marriage—since that is in effect what I have agreed to—will have one of two possible outcomes. Either the Frog will become himself, or he will refuse to become himself. In the first· instance, our children will be wholly human, and no doubt beautiful as well. In the second instance, you can all be absolutely certain that as long as His Stubborn Highness remains a frog, I will never allow him to be physically intimate with me. The very thought of it! Ugh!"

"So there will be no grandchildren?" the Queen said.

"Certainly not any half-frog, half-human ones."

"But what about your promise to let him sleep in your bed?"

"I will keep my promise. He may sleep on the edge of my mattress."

"But surely the phrase *sleep in your bed* is a metaphor," the Queen said.

"Perhaps in a poem, Mamà, but not in a contract. If Monsieur Frog wanted something else, he should have asked for something else."

"You are right," the King said. "You must perform what you promised, but you are not obligated to do anything further."

"Are you sure you won't reconsider?" the Queen said. "He is really a rather handsome fellow once you get used to him. And since both your father and I come from bloodlines that have been tall for a thousand years, the difference in your heights would undoubtedly balance out in your children."

"No, Mamà. I know how much you want grandchildren, but I will not compromise on this."

"Then you are a dreamer," said the Queen, "and a foolish girl. What makes you think that this good frog is anything but what he seems?"

"Now, now, my love," the King said. "Please don't get yourself upset again. We have been through a lot today. We are all a bit on edge."

"Your Majesty," the Frog said, "may I make another point?"

"Certainly," said the King.

"Please excuse me for mentioning this," the Frog said, "but I am almost fainting with hunger."

"Oh, dear me," the King said. "How very inconsiderate of us. We must stop talking until our guest has eaten and drunk his fill. I could use a few sips of Burgundy myself."

In the ensuing silence, the Frog leaned over to the Princess's plate and watched, deeply moved, as she picked up the first of the flies with the tip of her golden spoon.

XXV

On Promises

Our story is proceeding quickly now toward its denouement. So, while the Frog is eating from the Princess's plate and drinking from her cup, while the King and the Queen are making their way, in thought-charged silence, through new, warm portions of the squab, then the lamb, the cheese, the fruit, the double-chocolate cake, the gelato-topped apple-and-almond tart, and the bountiful wines that reflect and play with each flavor, I would like to comment on the Princess's attitude toward her promise and on the nature of promises in general.

When someone promises you that he will perform an act, he is stating that he will stand by his
word. In a sense, he is stating that he will stand
inside his word: that the act has already been per-
formed, since only time stands between the performance and his statement. Statement and
performance are not two separate things, but two
stages of the same thing, like child and adult.
When he makes you a promise, he is assuring you
that however the world changes, his word will not
change. Thus, he is creating the future inside the
present.

Even more: he is creating the present inside the
present. He is establishing one stationary point
amid the infinite flux of events. This is as much an
esthetic act as a moral one. A work of art's depth
of commitment to its own rules is a measure of its
integrity.

What allows his promise to you is his promise
to himself. In knowing that he will keep his word
(not merely that he will do everything in his power
to keep it), he has given himself one of the most

precious of gifts: the freedom from "I can't." That is, the freedom to *become* the person who will be able to keep his word. This freedom is essential in marriage, which is based on the confluence of two promises, and which is an adventure of such difficulty and peril that if one had known, beforehand, one might never have dared to begin. Thus, in a time of crisis, when he is convinced that he can't keep the promise and yet is committed to it beyond the limits of who he thinks he is, the promise is his point of entry into his own depths.

The Princess is not hungry. She barely touches the squab, and takes just a few token bites of the other courses. From time to time she sees the Frog's long tongue spear a fly from the edge of her golden plate. But her attention is focused elsewhere.

She has promised to love him. And as she sits there, the enormity of the promise rises in her like the dawn: a brightness on the horizon of her mind. She has not been aware until now of how much she already does love him. When did it begin? At the well, with his first dear loving question? But whose heart would not go out to someone so admirable in so many ways? Admirable, capable, compassionate, a finder of deep lost things. And how strong his love for her is. How touched she feels by the fierceness of his resolve, by his persistence in overcoming so many obstacles in order to reach her. And by his modesty. His eloquence. And how skillful he has been with both her parents, not glib or intimidated like some of her other suitors, but respectful, courtly, firm in just the right way. And really, he is not as ugly as he seemed at first; he is even a rather attractive fellow once you get used to him, as the Queen, in her well-meaning, devious way, remarked.

But what kind of love has she promised him? *Philia*, to be sure. That much was explicit: to love him and take him as her best friend. How to act as his friend is the essential question, and she will have to deal with it soon, she knows. She will somehow have to deepen her vision of who he truly is in order for him to see it himself. He can't simply be resigned to spend the rest of his life in this frog's body. She will have to hold the vision *for* him. How? Well, for one thing, she will have to let go of her irritation, and stop acting as if his refusal to become a prince were a personal affront. It is not a refusal, after all; it is a failure of the imagination. Once she stops taking it personally, her intention will be much clearer. And she will be able to act as a truer friend: without any vested interest, and solely for his benefit. Her words will be a clear mirror that shows him to himself.

And *agapē*: she is sure that she has promised him this mode of love, which is contiguous with the outer regions of *philia.* To love someone from the perspective of the Tao, as if there were no past or future. *Agapē,* too, will require an adjustment of her attitude, since to love someone in this way means to realize that he is perfect, that every apparent flaw or inadequacy is an optical illusion. No future means that there is no Prince, or that the Prince is already manifest within the Frog. This will be difficult for her, but possible. To hold the two views at once: that the Frog must at all costs become a prince, and that he is perfect just the way he is. But she has practiced double vision before, and she knows that holding two contradictory views is like looking out of two eyes: the only way to achieve depth.

But what about erotic love? That is the crux of the problem. It is not the kind of love she promised—definitely not. It is not a love she *could* have promised, since no energy is freer and less subject to the will than *eros* is. And in different circumstances—if the Frog and she could simply be best friends, if they could share their intimacies and interests (what his interests are she can't begin to fathom), if they could walk and study and sing together—the absence of *eros* would not pose the slightest problem. But here again, her mother is right: *sleep in your bed* does have a certain metaphorical resonance to it. She has made this compact not only with a frog but with a prince. If her love is to be complete, if this is to be a real marriage and they are to be man and wife, not frog and wife, then *eros* must somehow be invited into their bedroom. She doesn't know how. Nor, since she is a virgin, can she say that she knows herself sexually. She has some sense of the unexplored bodily wildness in her. But as much as she needs to test her own limits, she has no intention of testing them with a moist little animal.

The apple-and-almond tart lies before her untouched. A liveried waiter comes to the table and, from a golden spout like a swan's neck, pours into her cup a stream of dark Abyssinian coffee. She picks up one lump of sugar and drops it in, then reaches for the cream.

XXVI

Moonlight in the Palace

Night has come. The chandeliers have been extinguished. A full moon shines into the palace through windows and under doors. The huge tapestries in the reception hall, the suits of armor, the Raphaels and Titians on the walls, the Persian carpets, the intricate parquet floors, are all awash in moonlight. The last servant has snuffed out the last candle and crept off to bed, yawning. There is no one on the great marble staircase but you and I.

Can you feel the cool stone on the soles of your feet? Have you noticed the balusters? Dryads, fauns, tritons, mermaids, whose pale marble faces seem almost flushed with pleasure. And the ceiling: who could have painted that panoply of stars? Careful. It is easy to lose your balance. Here, take my hand. We are more than halfway to the top. How small the chairs and the tables look from here!

Now we turn left, onto the blue-and-red Persian runner in the hallway, so soft between the toes. That is a Leonardo coming up on our right. And here is the royal bedroom. The King and the Queen are asleep. Their candles are out. They have drawn the curtains around their bed. Let us keep walking. Past the second-floor library. Past the map room. Past the music room. Ah, here it is. The Princess's bedroom. Yes, we can walk right into it. We don't need to open the door.

XXVII

The Problem

"But why not?" said the Frog. He was sitting on top of the bedspread at the foot of the Princess's bed. The Princess was lying diagonally across it, elbows bent and chin supported by her palms, in a cream-colored satin nightgown. It was a large, four-poster ebony bed hung with cloth-of-gold and red velvet, its pillowcases and sheets made of Belgian linen and embroidered along each edge with garlands of tiny red roses. Red-violet silk, in a design of intertwined silver-pink keys and serpents, covered the walls. Above the gold-handled cherrywood bureau hung Caravaggio's portrait of the Princess, a life-size version commissioned at the same time as the miniature that was still hidden and dry inside the golden ball.

"You know the reason," the Princess said.

"Let me hear it from you."

"All right. Once more. You may sleep at the foot of my bed. But you may not sleep by my side. I will not be physically intimate with you. I don't even like touching you."

"I am well aware of that," the Frog said, with a sigh.

"But I do love you. Do you know *that*?"

"I do. That is, I think I do."

"And I am glad to be your friend. And really, don't you have everything you wanted now? You should be very happy."

"I *am* happy."

"Well, for someone who is happy, you look awfully glum."

"You are right. I am happy, but I am miserable."

"Why?"

"I thought that once we carried out our agreement, I would have everything I wanted. And now I find that it isn't enough."

"It isn't?"

"No. I keep longing to get closer to you, to lie beside you, to lie *inside* you. The longing is so intense that I don't know how I will be able to bear it."

"Oh, dear. This is serious."

"And I feel so very ugly. Every time you shudder or draw back from me, it hurts. I know that you can't help it, but it hurts."

"I was afraid of something like this," said the Princess.

"You were?"

"Yes. I do love you, and I know that we will be the best of friends. But something is missing for me, too. It will be hard to continue in this way. It really isn't enough for either of us."

"Well, what do you suggest?"

The Princess glared at him. The glare wasn't large: a penknife this time rather than a sword. But she caught herself, and her look softened.

"Oh," said the Frog.

"I have already tried kissing you. We know that *that* doesn't work."

The Frog was silent. He felt something begin to vibrate inside his vocal sac. It wasn't air; it was anger.

"You always want me to be someone else!" he burst out. "It isn't fair! I can't help it that my body disgusts you. If I could change it into something beautiful I would. And how can you say you love me? What kind of love is it, when the me you really love is someone else? I am *not* a prince. Why can't you just love me for who I am?"

The Princess said nothing for a moment. Then, with great tenderness: "I do love you for who you are. I *admire* you for who you are."

"And yet your body doesn't love me."

"That is true. My body doesn't love you. I can't help that. It is not up to me."

"But where does that leave us? I am miserable, and you are unsatisfied."

"We are certainly in a pickle. And I don't want to handle it the way most of my relatives, the kings and queens of Europe, do."

"What way is that?"

"Oh," said the Princess, "they marry from obligation, because they have made political deals. And then they take lovers. It is a sorry business. How can they learn what love truly is?"

"Well, it wouldn't work for me," the Frog said. "You are the only female I could mate with. I have never been attracted to frogs."

"So you *must* become yourself. It is the only way."

"But how? What should I do? When you say that I am a prince, I don't have the faintest idea of what you are talking about."

The Princess took a deep breath. There had to

be a way to show the Frog what she saw inside him. "Let us try something," she said.

"What?"

"Trust me." She unbent her arms and lowered her face until it was on the same level as the Frog's face, and within six inches of it. "Look into my eyes now," she said.

The Frog concentrated his attention until he was aware of nothing in the world but the Princess's eyes. He could see inside them the small twin images of himself.

Time disappeared.

He kept looking.

XXVIII

The Kiss

(2)

"Something happened," said the Princess. She was sitting in the center of the bed. "What did you see?"

"I can't express it," the Frog said. "But something did happen."

"Tell me, tell me! What was it?"

"Well, at first I felt as if I were completely surrounded by your eyes. Your vision was a pool of clear water, and I was breathing it into myself through all my pores. Was it your vision, or your love? They seemed like the same thing. They—it—was glorious. And then, just for an instant, I felt something stir in me, as if I were waking from a long sleep."

"What? Tell me! What was it?"

"I can't say. It was a kind of vastness. Some part of me, a part that was greater than the whole, and beautiful beyond words. And then I was aware of something else, something different from love, that was coming toward me through your eyes."

"Yes?"

The Frog blushed: a greenish red. "It was desire."

The Princess blushed.

"And I understood," the Frog said. "That is, I think I understood."

"You did? You do?"

"I saw what you have been talking about. That is, I think I saw. I *am* a prince, perhaps. I may very well be a prince. You may very well be right."

"Of course I am right!" the Princess said. "I have been telling you all along! Well, at least you believe me now."

"I *think* I believe you. I only had a glimpse, you know. It is very confusing."

"But now, at least, you don't have your heels dug in."

"But we are still in the same pickle," the Frog said. "The question remains, What are we to do?"

"I have an idea. Close your eyes."

The Princess leaned over, steadying herself on her elbow, and lowered her head until she was face to face with the Frog. Then she kissed him, tenderly, with a shudder, on his cold lips.

The Frog waited a few moments before opening his eyes. "Nothing?" he said.

"Nothing," said the Princess.

"I am so sorry," the Frog said. "It must have been unpleasant for you."

"Oh, it wasn't that unpleasant. I didn't mind."

"Well, I am very touched."

The Princess nodded.

"What now?" the Frog said.

"I don't know," said the Princess. "I really don't know."

XXIX

At the Edge

The Princess is sitting at the edge of the bed. She knows that something drastic is called for.

A transformation. There must be a transformation. But how? To break all patterns. To shatter all forms. To throw the world away and arrive on the other side of everything we know.

But how?

How?

XXX

Still at the Edge

The Princess is sitting at the edge of the bed. The Frog is sitting next to her. They are staring at the floor. They have no idea what to do next. They are waiting for something to happen.

They have almost come to the end of their story, yet the end is nowhere in sight. It seems unreachable.

The Frog is in a state of suspended animation—which, however, doesn't help at all. His eyes are glazed over. His nostrils are shut. He has sunk into hopelessness as if it were a dark winter pool from which he will never emerge.

The Princess is as desperate as he is. She has exhausted all possible solutions. Her mind refuses to make any further effort. She feels an immense weariness of heart. They are so close to a happy ending, yet infinitely far away. She can see the Frog sinking deeper and deeper. She has nothing left to give him. There is nothing further she can do. The rest is not up to her. But she cannot let go. There is too much at stake.

She lifts her head and glares into the distance. She is desperate, and wild with frustration. She knows that the author of her predicament is nowhere to be found, at least not outside herself. She also knows that there must be an answer, waiting for her somewhere, inaccessible.

How can she reach it? How in the world can she reach it?

Do you have the patience to wait / till your mud settles and the water is clear? / Can you remain unmoving / till the right action arises by itself?

Oh, shut up.

XXXI

Movement

Yes. She can sense it. There is movement. There is an infinitesimal stirring, deep down in the mind's darkness. She doesn't know what it is. But something is happening.

XXXII

Not Pity, but Compassion

People often confuse compassion with pity. Compassion is a mode of love. Pity is a mode of contempt.

Compassion sees us as we truly are, beyond excuses, beyond justification, beyond personality.

Compassion is pitiless.

XXXIII

The Answer

"I have it!" the Princess said, sitting bolt upright. "I have the answer!" There was an extremely resolute look on her face.

"Really?" the Frog said. "That is wonderful. Tell me."

"I can't believe it!" the Princess said. "It was so obvious! Listen: What you must do is trust me completely. What *I* must do is pick you up and throw you against the wall."

The Frog swallowed hard.

"It is the only way," the Princess said. There was not the slightest doubt in her voice.

"But isn't it perhaps a rather . . . forceful method?" said the Frog.

"It *is* forceful. But it will work. I know that it will work. And there is no other way."

"What about just letting me live with you for a while? Perhaps little by little I will absorb your vision and set myself free. And if that doesn't work, we can always try a more forceful method later."

"No, I don't think so. What is the life expectancy of a frog, after all? Six months? A year?"

"I don't know."

"Well, it can't be very long. If we were to try a slower method, you would be dead before we knew it. Even if the method worked, by that time you might very well be an old frog, and you would be transformed into an old man. And what good would that do me?"

"Oh," said the Frog.

"Anyway," the Princess said, "it is always best to strike when the iron is hot."

"Forgive me, dear Princess, but that is easy for *you* to say. You are the one who is doing the striking."

"That is true. I admit it."

"But if your method doesn't work, it will kill me, won't it? It sounds as if you intend to throw me quite hard."

"With all my might."

"And there is no way that I will survive. All that I will be is a red stain on the wall, and a heap of broken bones."

"Yes, if the method fails. If it succeeds, of course, you will be a prince. *My* prince."

"But I will not survive that, either."

"True. You will no longer be yourself—that is, you will no longer be who you *think* you are. Either way, you must be ready to die."

"So it seems," said the Frog. He closed his eyes, then opened them. "I am afraid."

"Don't be afraid, dear Frog," the Princess said. "I know that it will work."

"But what if it doesn't?"

"Even if it doesn't work, you will be trading six months as a frog for the possibility of fifty years as my beloved prince and husband. It is a noble risk. I hope you will take it."

"Ah," said the Frog, brightening. "That is what I want more than anything in the world. I would be glad to undergo a death for that. I would give up more than one life if only I could win your love."

"Trust me. I was right about your being a prince, wasn't I?"

"Yes. I think so."

"Well, I am right about this, too."

"I am afraid, but I do trust you."

"Enough to let this happen?"

"Yes. I will let it happen. You do think it is for the best, don't you?"

"I *know* it is for the best."

"Then all right," the Frog said. "I have made my decision. You may pick me up."

"Good," said the Princess. "I am very glad."

"Then . . . Then this is the last time that you and I will see each other."

"Yes."

"Can we have a last moment together?"

"Yes, of course."

The Princess picked the Frog up, gently, in her right hand. They looked into each other's eyes.

"Goodbye," said the Frog. "I love you."

"And I love you," said the Princess. "That is why I am doing this. Are you still afraid?"

"Yes."

"I am a little afraid, too."

"Ah."

A few more moments passed.

"Are you ready?"

"Yes."

The Princess walked, slowly, to within three feet of the gold-handled bureau. There was a large empty stretch of wall to the left of her portrait. She placed her left foot in front of her, held her breath, pivoted on her right foot, leaned back, and threw. The Frog flew out of her hand: a greenish blur hurtling toward a violet background.

XXXIV

The View from Midair

All at once the enveloping warmth of the Princess's hand is gone in a rush of fear. He is within inches of her fingers, he can still see them in exquisite detail: white and long, with nails painted a deep cadmium red. But as he continues to watch, her hand grows smaller. He feels himself rushing through air, the wind whistles around him. "Relax," he says to himself. "Just let it happen." But even as his muscles ease, he can feel the fear pounding in his heart. He sees not only her hand now but her whole form, bare arms and cream-colored satin growing instant by instant smaller. He is grateful that she threw him in such a way that his eyes are facing her. He has no idea where he is in relation to the wall or how quickly it is approaching. Good: he doesn't want to brace himself for the impact. He wants to keep all those sensations at the back of his awareness—the fear, the speed, the pain that is about to tear through his body, any thoughts of a possible transformation. He can sense now that she is looking intently at him, from so far away, her arms hanging at her sides, her head just barely tilted. He wants to keep concentrating on her. On how fiercely beautiful she is. On how dearly he loves her.

XXXV

The End

(1)

And here we come to the end of our story. What happened afterward we know from the Condensed Version, and it is easy to fill in the details: upon hitting the wall, the Frog was transformed into the most handsome, intelligent, shapely-legged, courteous, spiritual of French princes, who, clothed in a simple yet elegant black velvet suit, landed on his two feet with the poise of an accomplished gymnast. The Princess had been right all along, as the Frog—pardon me, the Prince—acknowledged, with a gratitude that shone through "his beautiful, kind eyes." After that first, speechless moment, he swept her up in his arms and carried her to the bed, where they spent the rest of the night (in the intervals between half-hour-long kisses) talking about their past, their future, and their miraculous, delicious present. Morning came before they knew it. Hand in hand they walked down the great marble staircase and, after a celebratory breakfast with the King and Queen, having taken affectionate leave of them and of the ministers, the courtiers, the servants, and the Fool—who landed a parting quip, funny but in questionable taste, about frogs' tongues—they rode off together, through the forest, into their new life.

XXXVI

On Transformation

Most scientists — most grownups — don't believe in happy endings. They think that there is a universal drift toward disorder, and a conservation of disappointment, which, like energy, is neither created nor destroyed but only changes form. The end of the human story, they think, is lifeless flesh, or a lifeless planet hurtling through mindless space.

But in the soul's thermodynamics, every rule proves the exception, every end is a new beginning, and all things, at all times, are possible. The great transformations, the weddings at the end of the world, the awe-filled unveilings of our true identity, are always surrounded by joy, and the voice of the storyteller eases into his final words the way the members of an orchestra play the final notes, then put down their instruments and wait in the silence that surrounds the music.

There remains the question of meaning. A frog turns into a prince. A lost son is found. A queen long dead steps down from her pedestal, flushed with life. Is this wishful thinking? Whistling in the dark? And if it isn't, if such transformations are images of what can actually happen to us, in us, what do they entail? What do they look and feel like?

Researchers recently studied a number of ex-frogs who are now handsome, happily married princes (a necessarily small number since, as the philosopher says, all things excellent are as difficult as they are rare). These ex-frogs were unanimous in their accounts. The great transformation, they said, had three requirements: a sustained not-knowing, the willingness to be thrown against a wall, and, always, the love of a visionary woman. And a fourth requirement: patience. Yes, an enormous patience, since the interval between the being-thrown and the actual impact may last for a decade or more.

These were modest men, who did not take their physical beauty for granted. It was a gift, they said, from a universe that delights in conforming to a lover's vision. All, without exception, spoke of the transformation itself with awe. One of them compared it to Adam's dream, who awoke and found it truth.

Looking back at their former selves from their present perspective was a poignant experience for them. Each could appreciate who he had once been, and was grateful for his froggish love and persistence. But each, lacking the kind of continuity that most of us feel when we remember the child we used to be, could barely recognize himself back then. A cataclysmic event had separated him from his former self; he both was and wasn't that self; he had been, as it were, reincarnated in a higher mode of existence, like the final, almost unrecognizably rich variation on a simple theme.

Sometimes on a summer evening, one prince said, as he walked with his beloved on a country lane with the ancient chorus of the frogs all around them, he would be jolted by an emotion halfway between laughter and tears, and he would have to stop, turn to his beloved, and find himself again in her eyes.

XXXVII

The End

(2)

The story of the Princess and the Frog ends at the moment of impact. What happens after that moment concerns the Princess and the Prince. I admit that it would be interesting to follow them as they ride away from the palace and into their new life. The sixteenth century is, after all, about to end. In less than a decade, the last of the Unusual Phenomena will have occurred. Again and again, in a marriage that keeps ripening and growing deeper over the course of fifty years, both of them will have to find ways of redefining the miraculous. Again and again they will each have to realize that *Happily ever after* doesn't begin with *Once upon a time:* it begins with Now.

But that is another story.